SAY IT WITH FLOWERS

Daisy Jones has abandoned her hectic London life for a more peaceful existence in her old home town. Taking on a florist's business is another huge gamble, but she loves it and the people she meets. Her new life brings a new love and her life looks set for happiness . . . until the complications set in. Nothing is quite what it seems and she sets off on an emotional roller coaster. Who said life in a small town is peaceful?

CHRISSIE LOVEDAY

SAY IT WITH FLOWERS

Complete and Unabridged

LINFORD
Leicester

First published in Great Britain in 2005

First Linford Edition
published 2006

British Library CIP Data

Loveday, Chrissie
  Say it with flowers.—Large print ed.—
Linford romance library
  1. Love stories
  2. Large type books
  I. Title
  823.9'14 [F]

  ISBN 1–84617–220–9

Published by
F. A. Thorpe (Publishing)
Anstey, Leicestershire

Set by Words & Graphics Ltd.
Anstey, Leicestershire
Printed and bound in Great Britain by
T. J. International Ltd., Padstow, Cornwall

This book is printed on acid-free paper

1

'Can you get the carnations out first, please?' Daisy called to her treasured helper, Barbara.

'Any particular colour?'

'She wants pinks. Imaginative eh?'

'Nothing wrong with pink. Hang on. McKay's are here with the order.'

'Blast. Rotten timing. I really need to get this arrangement done and out. It's her mum's birthday and she wants it to be there as a surprise when she gets up.'

'I'll see to McKay's. Is the order on the desk, for checking?'

'Should be.' Daisy busied herself collecting pieces of green foliage and a few sprigs of gypsophila for fillers, to bulk out and set off the coloured blooms. The pink carnations and spray carnations were still in the cold room, kept there overnight for

1

freshness. She pulled down a basket from the shelf and taped the wet oasis in place.

She loved making arrangements almost more than any other part of her routine. Base of foliage, nothing too heavy or dramatic but something to complement the flowers and most of all, something that would please her elderly customer.

As she worked, she watched as Barbara talked to the delivery man. The older woman was brilliant with people. Customers, suppliers, hard-to-please women, uncertain men and nervous brides. She dealt with them all and usually managed to raise a smile before they left the little shop.

'That's coming on nicely. I'll start getting the flowers in water, shall I?'

'Thanks.' Daisy was absorbed in her work, almost finishing her pretty little basket, but standing back, thinking it lacked something. A few sprigs of statice. Deep purple would set off the pink carnations to perfection. She noted the extra pieces used on the little pad she kept by her, ready for the final costing.

It was all too easy to put in a bit of this or that and find at the end of the day, a large number of items had been used up without being charged. There was scant enough profit as it was, but her reputation for high-quality flowers was building. She added up the items and grimaced slightly. Even at cost price, it seemed a lot of money. But, the woman who'd ordered her mother's present could afford it and it was probably an easy way out for her to send something like this.

Barbara was whistling as she filled up the containers with nutryl solution, a special nutrient to keep cut flowers fresh for as long as possible. She was always whistling or singing. It was probably down to her that the business was successful.

'Finished. Do you want to deliver it or shall I?'

'Don't mind, love. I can get on here,

if you fancy a little outing,' Barbara said.

'I'll take it then, if you're really sure. It's a lovely day and it isn't far. Down by Cutler's Farm somewhere, isn't it?'

'I reckon it's one of the old folks' bungalows they built next to the farm.'

'Come on then, Emma. Let's go.' The little Jack Russell followed her out of the office, her tail wagging in delight at being offered an outing.

Daisy went to the little van parked to one side of the shop. It was lucky for them there had been a slight gap between the shops as parking spaces were like gold dust in this part of town. They always had to stretch a rope across the gap when the van went out or someone else would have taken the spot, causing endless hassle.

She drove out and waved her thanks as Barbara put the rope back. Just a couple of minutes later, she was leaving the little market town and heading for the country close by. She sniffed the spring air through the open window

4

and once more rejoiced in the changes in her life.

It had seemed like such a huge gamble to give up her hectic London lifestyle for this comparatively slow and gentle pace of life. A huge drop in her finances, too. Working for an advertising agency had meant long hours, a frantic pace and never any time to spend doing things for herself.

There were always parties, launches of new products, entertaining clients . . . something to take up her time. All her old friends had thought she was potty to bury herself in a florist's shop in a town that no-one had even heard of. But she knew it had been the right thing to do.

When she had broken off her engagement to Ray, she needed to get away. He'd called her a drama queen when she told him she was leaving, but in her heart, she'd known they weren't right for each other.

'Sorry Raymond, but I simply couldn't keep up the pace,' she muttered aloud. It wasn't really him she was missing but just having someone special to spend time with. Besides Emma, of course. The little dog looked up at her and as always, wagged her tail.

She reached the turning to the farm and drove along the bumpy track. This couldn't be right. She must have missed the correct lane. She could see someone working in the yard and stopped the van.

'Excuse me, I seem to have got myself lost. I'm looking for Cutler's cottages.'

The man stood up and walked over to the van. He was younger than she'd at first thought. A small dog ran over barking. Another Jack Russell. Emma put her paws on the window and barked back.

'You've taken the turning a bit too early. It's the next lane you come to, on the main road. Florist, eh? You're about to make someone very happy, no doubt. Crazy Daisy? Are you the one who's taken over at Anita's?'

'Yes. I've been there almost eight months now.'

'Going well is it?'

'Not bad. Now, if you'll excuse me, I'd better get on. Before my dog decides she's totally in love with yours and disgraces me completely.' He laughed, showing a row of pure white, even teeth. His brown eyes crinkled at the corners as he guided her round the narrow turning point.

'I'll see you again,' he called. 'Ben Ciammo.'

'Pleased to meet you, Ben Ciammo. That has to be Italian.'

'My grandparents came over here years ago. I'm all British though, apart from the name.'

'I'm boring old Daisy Jones. Also all British.'

'Pleased to meet you, boring old Daisy Jones. And your friend? The four-legged one?'

'She's Emma. One year old and a total flirt. Now, I'm sorry, but I really do have to get on. Thanks for your help.' He stood back and watched as she drove back up the narrow lane.

She looked through the driving mirror and saw him still standing watching. He raised a hand in salute. She waved back, wondering if he could possibly have seen her. He was nice she reflected. Very nice but undoubtedly married and probably the father of several children. At least.

* * *

'Happy Birthday, Mrs Herbert,' she said when the old lady opened her door.

'Oh my dear, how perfectly lovely. Oh aren't they just gorgeous and my favourite colour too. Won't you come in?'

'I'm sorry, but I have to get on. They're from your daughter. She wrote you a little card, see?'

'Kind of her, I'm sure. But it was surely your creative flair that made such a pretty arrangement? My daughter couldn't put anything in a vase and make it look half decent. Are you sure you haven't time for a cup of tea? I've only just made a pot.'

'Oh, go on then. I really shouldn't, but as it's a special occasion. Just a few minutes.' Daisy hoped that Barbara wasn't too busy but the old lady was so keen for her to talk.

The tiny sitting-room was cosy and warm and filled with pictures of presumably, her children and grand-children.

'I've been so lucky,' she said. 'Cards from everyone. It's nice they all remember my birthday.'

'And will they be coming to see you?' Daisy asked. She bit her lip. That was tactless, she realised.

'I expect they are all much too busy to have time to come all the way over here to see me. They have such exciting lives, you know. All young people do nowadays.'

'I really mustn't stop for long,' Daisy

said, hoping she would take the hint and pour the tea. 'My colleague in the shop will be sending out a search party.'

'You're such a pretty young girl. Nice to know that not all young people live in a whirl of going here and there. And that you have such talent. Few people can arrange flowers so beautifully these days.'

'I must get it from my mother. She was always wonderful with flowers and she must have passed her love of them on to me.'

It was ten minutes before Daisy could make her escape. The delivery had taken half an hour, which she took into account the chat with Ben. But, heck, she was her own boss and Mrs Herbert was smiling so happily when she left. Her only guilt was if Barbara had been busy and was cursing her for being away so long.

'So I needn't have phoned the police after all,' Barbara said as Daisy went into the shop.

'Sorry. Mrs Herbert was all alone on

her birthday, surrounded by expensive cards and greetings and with no hope of seeing a soul. I just had to have a cup of tea with her.'

'You're a kind soul. Bet you made her day. Hasn't been much going on here. One of those planted bulb baskets and a few bunches of daffs.'

'Take heart. It's Mother's Day soon. You can get your creative juices flowing again for that.'

'I'll put the kettle on,' Barbara said with a frown. 'Why we can't spread Mother's Day out over the year, I'll never know.'

'You know anything about the bloke at Cutler's Farm?' Daisy asked as innocently as she could.

'Not really. Heard they were an Italian family. Grow mainly tomatoes don't they? Hardly a farm really. More a sort of market garden. Why?'

'Just wondered. I took the wrong turning and ended up in his yard. He's got a Jackie like Emma. She seemed very smitten.'

'Oh really?' Barbara replied with a grin on her face. It was about time her young boss showed some interest in the opposite sex. 'And it was him that brought the sparkle to your eyes I expect.'

'What sparkle? Don't be silly. And you can take that grin off your face. I don't have any time for men in my life. I'm far too busy organising the business. Besides, I'm sure that someone with Ben's looks is well and truly married. Probably got a large family as well. You know how these Italians are.'

'I'll see what I can find out,' Barbara promised gleefully. 'Now, are you going to sort out these flowers or do I have to do that as well?'

Daisy shrugged and began to snip the stems and arrange the various sprays in the tall vases. Gone were the days when a few daffodils were enough for the spring market. Nowadays, people expected exactly what they wanted to be available at all times.

The shop bell jangled.

'Good morning. How can I help?' she asked the middle-aged lady who was staring at the many vases of flowers.

'Oh dear. I don't know. I thought I'd like a bunch of something to cheer me up but there are so many lovely colours here, I don't know what to choose. I expect they're all beyond my means.'

Daisy frowned. It must be something about the way they were displayed. Several of her clients expressed the thought that they were spoilt for choice. She eyed the lady and steered her towards the inexpensive sprays of carnations. There were several colours and with a bit of greenery, they'd make a pretty vase and usually lasted for several days.

'What colour is your room?' she asked the lady.

'Rather drab beige, I'm afraid.'

'Then you need something fairly bright. How about these?' She held out a bunch of orange-tipped blooms, a creamy yellow at the base. 'And a piece of this green foliage with it would just set it off nicely.'

'That sounds lovely. Thank you dear. How much would that be?'

The woman looked delighted at the sum mentioned and fished out her purse immediately. As she left the shop with her flowers nicely wrapped in cellophane she turned back and smiled.

'Thank you so much for taking such trouble for me. Especially as it was such an inexpensive purchase.'

'Don't mention it. I'm pleased to help.'

The pace of work speeded up as the morning progressed. Both women were kept busy serving, making up bouquets and arrangements and answering the phone. They were part of a national network of florists and every now and again, the computer would hum as a new order was sent to them.

'Now, I'm off out with the next deliveries. There are about three in the town and then a couple out on the Northfield Estate,' Barbara said.

Alone in the shop, Daisy busied

herself with tidying up and sorting orders. There was always something to do. The bell clanged as the door opened. Her heart gave a small leap as she saw it was Ben.

'Oh, hi. Can I help?'

'Hello again. I want some flowers please. A bouquet of some sort. To say sorry. What do you suggest?' He leaned on the counter, bringing his eyes to her level. There was a slight sound behind her and she saw Emma pattering into the shop.

'Emma, go back. You know you're not allowed out here.' The little dog looked woebegone and turned back, her tail tucked somewhere between her back legs. 'I can't imagine why she came out. She never stirs usually.'

'Maybe she recognised my voice from this morning. Perhaps she thought I'd brought Toby with me.'

'Maybe. Now, flowers. What price were you thinking of?'

'No idea. What do you think?'

'Depends how sorry you are.'

He laughed. 'Ingratiatingly sorry. I blew it big time.'

'A lady I presume?' He nodded. 'A special lady?'

'They don't come any more special.'

'Help me out here. Do you want an arrangement? A bouquet? What sort of colours?'

'Something cheerful. A bouquet might need her to spend time arranging it, so maybe an arrangement would be a good idea. Bright reds, I think.'

'OK. Do you want to wait? Or have it delivered?'

'I'll wait if that's OK. If you don't mind my watching you at work, that is.'

Daisy didn't mind at all. It meant she spent a bit longer in his company. Then she paused. He was buying flowers for a special lady, no-one more special, he'd said. To apologise for something he'd done. Why then, was her heart fluttering like a bird in a cage? Why was he actually flirting with her? That's what he was doing wasn't it? The way he was

16

leaning near to her, the way he was smiling and watching her every movement. She drew in her breath and began to collect the materials together, trying to look as professional as possible.

'So, Daisy Jones. What's your story?' he asked lazily, sounding as if he was actually interested, she thought.

'Nothing much. I lived near here when I was a child and now I've come back.'

'No rings, I notice. Does that mean there isn't a Mr Jones lurking in the background?'

'Shall I mix the reds with some orange and maybe a dash of purple? That would make a very clear statement, don't you think?'

'Exactly what would it be stating?'

'That you are sorry but ready to move forward. You don't want to stay miserable and the colours are vibrant with a life to be lived.'

'Wow! A psychologist as well. I hope the message is as clear to the recipient.

Do I get a card to write with the flowers?'

'Certainly. I'd suggest one of these.' She handed him a flower picture, one she had actually taken herself and had made up into cards on her computer. He studied it and nodded.

'That's fine. Can I borrow a pen?' He scrawled something she couldn't manage to see, despite craning her neck around. He stuffed it in the tiny envelope and she put it on a plastic spike and stuck it into the arrangement. He stared at the flowers and smiled. His face seemed to light up and she felt her heart turn over yet again.

This man was having a very strange effect on her. Pity he was sending flowers to someone else. She worked on his arrangement and tried to talk as she would to any other customer. Emma was still hanging around, just inside the door of the preparation room.

'Can't she come and say hello?' Ben asked.

'Oh, all right. Just this once. You

obviously have some magic ingredient that's drawing her to you. Perhaps she can smell your little dog. What did you say his name was?'

'Toby. She's obviously fallen in love at first sight. Maybe we should let them go out together one day.' He picked up the little dog and petted her. She settled in his arms in a way she had never seen her do before.

'Maybe. I'm not sure if it's a good idea. There, your flowers are ready. Will that do?'

'It's beautiful. Thank you.' He took out his wallet and peeled off a couple of ten pound notes. She held out his change but he shook his head. 'That's OK. Thanks for letting me stay and talk. I'll see you again soon.'

2

The image of Ben Ciammo kept popping into Daisy's mind at the most unlikely moments. Two days later, Barbara was convinced she was sickening for something and kept asking if she needed anything like paracetamol or throat pastilles.

'I'm fine. Honestly. Stop worrying. Now, I think it's my turn to make the deliveries today. I'll finish the bouquet for the bank and then I'll be off. Come on, Emma.'

She drove into the road and set off to the next town to make her deliveries. Things seemed to have changed so much since she'd lived there as a child and many of the roads looked quite different. So many new houses had been built; she often wondered where all the people had come from. Though it was well into March, it was still quite chilly and she was pleased to get back to the shop and relative warmth.

'You missed a customer,' Barbara said triumphantly when she returned.

'Really? More than one I hope.'

'A gentleman. Very keen to see you specially, he said.'

'Oh yes? Who was that?' She tried to sound casual, but something told her she knew exactly who the customer had been.

'Ben Chi-whatsit,' she said. 'Wanted you to make up a bouquet for him. Said he'd call back later as he really wanted you to do it yourself. Something about psychology, he said. I didn't know what he was on about, but I said you wouldn't be long. He's coming back later.'

Daisy frowned. What was he playing at? If he was buying flowers for someone so often, he could hardly be interested in her.

'You're incorrigible, Barb. Is match-maker your middle name?'

'Just like to see everyone happy.'

'If he's buying flowers for someone else, he's hardly going to be available, now is he?' Daisy pointed out.

'Could be for his mother.'

'Or his fiancée. You don't buy expensive flowers to say you're sorry to your mother. Mums just understand, don't they?'

'You've lost me.'

She explained about Ben's visit a couple of days earlier. She looked up and saw his tall outline against the door. She tried to look casual but was aware that her heart was beating a little faster than usual. What was it about this man?

'Hello. Back so soon?'

'I needed some flowers. For a lady. To say thank you. How's Emma? I've brought Toby to see her.'

'I don't encourage dogs in the shop,' Daisy said a trifle sharply.

'But these two are destined to be very good friends. Look, Toby's scented her already.'

'You're crazy,' she said, laughing.

'OK. I give in. Put Toby down and he can go through to the back.' Ben smiled again. She felt as if the sun had come out suddenly. 'So, it's flowers to say thank you. To a lady. Young or old?'

'Youngish. But not too young. About your age.'

'I see. And what sort of thing does she like? Roses? Lilies? Carnations?'

'I really don't know. She's been very good to me and I wanted to say thank you. That's what you do isn't it? Say it with flowers?'

Daisy didn't much like the idea of anyone being very good to him, but, he was just a customer and she needed every bit of trade she could get.

'What are your favourite flowers? Maybe that's the way to play it.'

'With a name like mine? Anything daisy-like. I suppose gerberas are just about my favourites. Or we do have some nice roses. Red ones? They mean love, you know. Or yellow ones perhaps?'

'Just make up a nice bunch for me.

With a pretty bow on it. Make it look special. Whatever you think.'

She laid the longer stems on the counter and arranged the rest on top. She bound it with raffia and tore off a sheet of cellophane. He watched her intently and then glanced down as the two Jack Russells came tearing out of the back room, chasing each other as if their lives depended on it.

Emma went down on her front paws, teasing and baiting Toby until he leapt at her, tail wagging nineteen to the dozen. Emma took a flying leap out of his way and crashed into a vase of tall white lilies. It fell over and knocked into a vase of long-stemmed roses.

'Stop it,' she screamed. 'Emma. Heel.' She was furious and snatched her dog from the chaos. 'Get in the office and stay there,' she ordered. 'Trust them to choose the most expensive flowers. Typical.' Ben had gathered his dog into his arms and stood looking anxious.

'I'm really sorry. They were only playing. I'll pay for the damage of course.'

'It wasn't your fault. I shouldn't have let even small maniacs like those two, loose in the shop.' She picked up the damaged blooms and laid them on the counter. 'I may be able to use some of them in an arrangement. It's only the stems that are broken. The heads are OK. Except that one,' she said pulling off a rose with a two inch stem. 'Here. Have a buttonhole as a souvenir.' He took it and held it in his hand awkwardly.

Quickly, she twisted the florist's ribbon into a bow and fastened it off with a piece of wire, attaching it to the base of the wrapping on his bouquet. She taped a pack of nutryl to the paper and handed it over.

'You are very clever,' Ben told her. 'Watching you make that bow was amazing. You make it look so simple. I'm sure she'll be delighted with the flowers. Thank you.'

'You haven't written a card,' she reminded him.

'It's OK. I'm taking them right now, anyway. I'm really sorry about the mess. We'd better meet in an open space next time. How about going for a walk on the common one evening?'

'Oh, I'm not sure. I'll think about it.'

'It's only fair to the dogs. They've obviously taken to each other and it would be cruel to keep them apart now wouldn't it?'

'Maybe,' Daisy replied doubtfully. She mustn't get personally involved. Now with a man who was always buying flowers for other women, however good it was for the business.

'I'll give you a call. Bye now. Thanks again for the flowers.'

Barbara came in from the back room.

'What on earth was all the noise about? Was it those dogs? I didn't like to come through before in case you were discussing something private. Oh, my dear lord. What a mess. Water everywhere. And how many flowers

26

have they ruined?' She began to salvage what she could before fetching the mop and bucket to begin to dry the floor.

'Thanks, Barb. It was obviously a mistake to let the dogs play in this place. I've never seen Emma go quite so potty.'

'She's obviously smitten. You'll have to meet out somewhere and go for a walk.'

'He suggested that. I dunno. He's buying flowers for a woman, so he must have someone in his life.'

'I'm just suggesting he goes for a walk with you and your dog. Nothing else. No life sentence.'

'No. Of course not.' Daisy blushed and mopped frantically at the water, trying to cover her embarrassment. She had to admit, she did find Ben very attractive but her commonsense told her that she needed to play it down a little. After the major disaster with Raymond, she really shouldn't even think of being interested in any other men.

She gave a little sigh. If Ray had had his way, they'd probably be married by now and producing babies. Though the idea of babies appealed to her greatly, it had to be with the right man.

However much she'd liked Ray, they'd never shared the sort of love she'd longed for.

'So, what do you think?' Barbara was saying. 'Come on girl. Where are you?'

'Sorry. I was miles away. What did you say?'

'Something was upsetting you all right. You were stabbing at that floor as if it was a lifelong enemy. How about a nice cuppa?'

'Great. I'll put the kettle on.'

There were a few more customers, but nothing to keep them too busy. Barbara began to wash out all the vases and bleach them ready for the new delivery the next morning. It was a long-winded process but very necessary to keep everything free of bacteria and cross-contamination.

'There's something coming through

on the National Flower Network. I thought we might finish a bit early this evening but looks like I was wrong.' Daisy went to look at the new order that had just arrived.

'It's for tomorrow. That's OK. Oh dear. Two funeral posies. A double one for the coffin. White lilies of course. Hope the order comes in early in the morning. We're nearly out of lilies, thanks to my dear little puppy.' Emma looked up and wagged her tail. She seemed to be aware of the fact that she was in disgrace. 'Yes, you need look ashamed of yourself. Behaving like that in front of a gentleman caller.'

'You might be able to use some of the lilies we've got left after Emma's little rampage. You really only need the heads and it's the long stems that are damaged.' Barbara was right. It wasn't all loss.

'You doing anything nice this evening?' Daisy asked.

'It's my soaps night tonight. I'll doubtless fall asleep after that, in front of the telly. I usually do after a busy day. What about you?'

'Nothing much. I'll catch up on some paperwork, I think.'

'You should get out and about. Youngster like you shouldn't be in sitting in front of a computer. Get out and enjoy yourself.'

She sorted out the flowers she would need in the morning and put them into one container. She then dumped several pieces of the shaped oasis in water. It was rather short notice for something as complicated as this, especially as they were needed by soon after ten the next day. But as always, she knew she would cope. All the same, she would have to be in early to get the work completed.

The wonderful Barbara would sort out the routine stuff in the morning while she worked. She locked the shop and got into the little van. Usually, she walked home with Emma, to give them both some exercise but as she had had an early start, the extra time saved would be vital.

Just as she was pulling away, she saw a Land Rover rushing towards her. She braked, wondering what maniac was driving at that pace through this narrow street. It stopped behind her, blocking the way. To her surprise, Ben climbed out.

'Come on. We're going to the common. I thought as it was such a lovely evening, we should do it right away.'

'But it'll be dark soon and I've got a load of work to do. Besides, I'm starving. And you're causing a traffic jam.' A couple of cars were hooting behind him.

'Then you'd better say yes pretty smartly or your name will be mud in this town. Come on. Follow me. Then I'll treat you to a cottage pie at the pub. They're world famous, you know.'

'You're mad. But, OK. For the sake of peace in our town, I'll follow you out.' She sighed and asked herself why she was being so foolish as to go along with him. Emma yapped and her tail was flying like a little windmill. 'OK. So you want us to double date, do you?' she said. Emma yapped again as Daisy steered the van out into the stream of traffic, wondering exactly what she was letting herself in for.

Ben was waiting for her to catch up along the road, obviously making sure she was following, she assumed. She flashed the headlights and he moved off.

Soon, they were driving down the narrow lane that lead to the old common where she'd played as a child. Instead of the old, rough tufts of grass and sandy patches, it was now a smooth field with goal posts and nothing else in the way of character. She hadn't been there for years and felt a sense of loss at the changes.

Quite out of character, Emma was scrabbling to get out of the van. She had spotted Toby charging towards them. She laughed and opened the passenger door. Immediately, the pair charged over the grass, barking and leaping with delight.

'It's really weird,' she said to Ben. 'I've never seen her behave like this before, with any other dog.'

'Like I said, love at first sight. They're obviously destined to make perfect parents. Unless she's been spayed of course.'

'No, but I'm hardly planning on letting her have any pups. Life's complicated enough without all that to contend with.'

'And don't you believe in love at first sight?'

'Not really. I think it takes time to get to know someone. You can get quite wrong first impressions.' She was thinking of Ray. He'd swept her off her feet and at first, she could hardly believe her luck that he seemed to have chosen her. As the months went on, she realised he was completely self-obsessed. He was good looking and dressed well, but spent hours achieving the look he wanted. Initially, she'd thought he was so special in

33

wanting to look his best.

'So, first impressions of me?'

She came back to the common with a start. 'Oh. Nice. Thoughtful, obviously. Buying the flowers, I mean. You obviously love your dog. That's about it. I don't know anything else about you except your father's Italian. You certainly have the dark looks of an Italian.'

'And is that good? I mean, do you like dark men?'

'I've never really thought about it. I usually like the man for what he is, rather than how he looks.'

'How very unusual. I certainly like what I see.'

'Oh yes? And what's that?'

'A beautiful blonde. Perfect teeth, neat competent hands. Lovely figure. A thoughtful person with possibly a strong sense of humour. At least, I hope so.' She followed his gaze. Emma and Toby were racing towards them, looking very pleased with themselves. They were also both now dark brown and smelled appalling.

'You little horrors. Where've you been?'

'I guess there were some horses over here recently. We should throw them both in the pond. That has to smell better than this. How could you lead my poor innocent little Toby astray, you sinful woman?' Emma leapt up, wagging her tail even faster.

'Emma's never done that before. It's your wretched Toby that's leading her astray!'

'Pond it is then. We'll put them both in the back of my Land Rover and we'll go and get something to eat. They can sit it out in the back. Can't have them stinking out your flower van. Doesn't go with the image.'

'I'm not sure we should trust them together, in the first place. There's been nothing but trouble since we met. Anyhow, don't you have a wife to get back to?'

'I'm a free man tonight. No wife. No commitments. Well, not until later.'

'OK. We'll risk it.' She wondered

about his words. The 'not until later', rang in her ears. 'But I mustn't be too late. Besides, that disgusting wretch does actually have to be fed as well. Though she doesn't deserve it.'

'They were only having fun. Doing dog stuff. Chill out. To the pond,' he ended with a shout. Unceremoniously, he picked up each dog in turn and flung it into the duck pond, where as a child, Daisy had come with bags of crumbs to feed her favourite ducks. The dogs swam back to the shore frantically, yapping with delight as they splashed along. They leapt out and shook themselves violently, racing off down the lane once more.

'Come back here,' Ben yelled. As one animal, they swerved round and galloped back to him. 'Now then, you can both get in the back there and stay there until you've dried out. At least the worst of it's washed off,' he said apologetically. 'Now, will you follow me again?'

They drove to the little pub near the

common and parked side by side. Emma lay down, close to Toby, almost looking as if she was challenging Daisy not to separate her from her new friend.

'It's OK, girl. You can stay there for now. But any more damage and you'll never see him again.' Toby stared at her and almost looked as if he was smiling. 'You too. Behave or you don't meet again.'

3

Ben was laughing as he took her arm and led her into the pub. She hadn't been there since her return to the little town and didn't know the landlord at all.

'What do you want to drink?' Ben asked.

'Glass of red wine please.'

'And I'll have a pint. It's been a hectic day. Have you met Daisy, by the way? She has the flower shop. Used to be Anita's. Now it's Crazy Daisy and really lives up to its name.'

'Hello there. I'm Will. Welcome to Brindley.'

'Thanks, but I was actually born here. My parents moved away many years go, but I was at school here.'

'Really? You might know my missus then. She went to the comprehensive. I'd have thought you are much of an age. Josie. Was Josie Robinson.'

'Good heavens. I should say so. We got up to all sorts of stuff together. How exciting. Is she in now?'

'She's putting the kids to bed. Be down in an hour or so.'

'Any chance of a couple of cottage pies?' Ben asked. Only we're both starving.'

'Sure. Josie got them all prepared and ready to cook, this afternoon.'

'Wow. She's actually cooking the food for the pub?' Daisy asked doubtfully. 'I remember some of our cookery lessons at school. Not to be recommended.'

'She went to catering college. You'd be surprised how she's come on, I'm sure.'

'Her cottage pies are legendary,' Ben assured her. 'Now, if you've finished reminiscing for awhile, I could do with a sit down.'

'Sorry. Only it's such a shock finding an old friend like that.'

'I hadn't realised you were a local girl.'

'I spent a lot of time in London, after uni. Worked there until I decided I'd had enough of the city life.'

She found him so easy to talk to that she'd almost told him her life story by the time their meal arrived. He had the knack of drawing information from her without letting slip any details of his own life. She told him about her parents who now lived in France. They'd gone over before the property boom, when prices were cheap and had a wonderful place in Provence.

'I expect you miss them, don't you?'

'Well, we phone each other every now and again and I visit for holidays of course, but we sort of stopped living in each other's pockets when I went to university.'

'And isn't a flower shop something of a let-down after the bright lights of London?'

'I love it. People here are real, not superficial like a lot of the media folk. Sorry, I'm going on a bit.'

She wanted to know more about him.

She still wasn't sure if he was single, she realised, after his somewhat enigmatic response to her enquiry about a wife. She tried again.

'So who were the flowers for?'

'Sorry, to someone whose birthday I'd missed and thank you, to someone who did a big favour for me.'

'Now, shall we have pudding or do you think we should rescue our hounds? Before they do anything else.'

'I was hoping to see Josie . . . but I can always give her a call. You're right. We should rescue the dogs and I do still have work to do.' Behind the bar, Will overheard her comment.

'I'm sorry. One of the kids is playing up. Josie won't be down just yet, I'm afraid. I told her you were here and she can't wait to see you.'

'Maybe another time?' Ben suggested. 'You know where to find Daisy, don't you? You could always buy your wife a bunch of flowers. I can recommend them. Work wonders with the ladies. And she's very good, our

41

Daisy. She'll give you exactly the right thing for the customer.'

'Thanks for the vote of confidence. Tell Josie I'll call her.' Daisy couldn't hide her grin at the compliment.

They went out and found the two dogs curled together as if they'd always shared a bed. 'Come on Emma,' Daisy called. Almost regretfully, she got up, stretched and shook herself and licked Toby's nose.

'Do I get a similar goodnight kiss?' asked Ben.

'I can lick your nose, if you really want me to.'

He pulled her close and gently kissed her lips. 'Goodnight Daisy Jones. See you soon.'

Daisy wasn't sure how she felt about it. It had been even nicer than she had expected, being kissed by Ben. But she still wasn't sure about him. Was he really unattached or had his enigmatic comment about having no ties until later, meant something more than he was letting on?

At eight o'clock the next morning, Daisy pulled into the tiny car park outside the shop. There were no people about and she let Emma run free to the door. She let herself in and switched off the alarm. She switched on the computer and checked the answering machine.

There was a message from Josie, saying how sorry she was to have missed her and promising they would catch up very soon.

She saw on the computer that there had been further orders for the funeral and immediately went into action. It would take a lot of hard work to get everything ready for ten o'clock. Barbara wouldn't be in till nine and the new delivery of flowers was due in half an hour.

She took out the necessary blooms from the store and began her work. National Flower Network provided pictures of exactly what was offered and each florist made up the posies, wreaths etc, as closely as possible to the specification. That way, nobody was disappointed and they knew exactly what the cost would be.

'Hi, Daisy,' called Barbara as the bell clattered, dismissing her moment's quiet reflection.

'You're early.'

'I knew you'd be busy and I thought I could at least take the flowers to the funeral directors for you.'

'Bless you. That was very good of you. I've got two more to do. Came in overnight.'

'Can't believe people can be so thoughtless. You'd think they'd know before this if they were going to need flowers. Can you manage with what flowers we've got?'

'McKay's should be here soon. I'm pushing it to make up one of the white lily sprays, as requested but the coffin top spray will be fine.'

'I'll get the bases soaked and some greenery sorted. You're making a lovely job of that one.' Barbara went into the back room and gathered the various

44

things they needed, setting them out on the bench ready for Daisy to pick up when she needed them. There was a sudden hammering at the door as the wholesaler arrived with the new order.

'Thank heavens,' Barbara called out as she busied herself with Mr McKay and the supplies. She carried the boxes through to the back of the shop and checked the invoice. Daisy worked steadily, concentrating on her task and saying little more than a brief hello.

'My, you're doing a lovely job there,' he told her as he walked past. 'You have a real flair for the flowers. Don't often see what happens to them after I've left them.'

'Thanks. Sorry I'm not stopping to chat this morning, but I've three more tributes to do before ten. I promise I'll make you a coffee next time.'

'No problem love. I'll see you next week.'

She pushed in the final sprigs and moved the arrangement to one side, contemplating it thoughtfully. She glanced at the picture in the National Flower Network book and nodded her approval.

'You know, I'd like us to do our own arrangements,' she muttered to Barbara. 'If I get the website sorted, we could have a similar sort of thing on there. Pictures and prices. We could make them much cheaper and better value. What do you think?'

'Not sure. It sounds like a lot of work and you'd still need the National Network for orders. They wouldn't like it if you went all independent on them.'

She nodded, and pulled the next lot of materials on to the workbench. By nine-thirty, she was ready to pack the van. Barbara was finishing arranging the new flowers into the various vases.

'I'll finish those, if you want to deliver this lot to Moss's.' The older woman nodded and took off her apron. Emma looked up hopefully as she saw the van's keys being removed from the hook. 'No, you're staying right here little dog. After your disgraceful behaviour last night, you don't get any treats today.'

'Oh? What happened?' Barbara asked. Daisy gave her a quick outline of the events and smiled at Barbara's expression.

'No need to look like that. We simply took the dogs out for a run and then had a bite to eat. That was it. Now are you going to deliver these flowers or do I have to do everything around here?'

There were several customers during the next half hour and Daisy was kept busy making up simple bouquets and wrapping the bunches of flowers needed.

A large woman came in. She was expensively dressed and had the air of someone used to having everyone dance attendance on her.

'Are these the only things you have for sale?' she asked.

'Did you want something special?' Daisy enquired.

'Well, certainly something better than

spray carnations. Anita used to get me special orders. The more exotic blooms. Bird of Paradise, various lilies. I must say, it's disappointing to think the shop has come down to these dreary-looking things.'

'I can get anything you require, madam. I don't carry the more exotic stock, as you put it, as there is little demand for it and I can neither abide nor afford waste.'

'Maybe I'll see what the other shop can offer.'

'Certainly, madam. And if we can help at all, well you only have to say. My wholesaler comes in on Mondays and Thursdays.'

'Thanks. I'll let you know.' With a cloud of expensive perfume, she swept out of the shop and out of sight. A woman about her own age came in and stood smiling at her.

'Daisy Jones. Who'd have thought it?' She stared for a moment and recognition dawned.

'Josie? Josie, how lovely to see you

again.' She went round the counter and hugged her old friend. For a moment, she had been at a loss as to who it was, but the eyes soon reminded her of the girl she'd once known at school.

'I couldn't wait to see you. I've abandoned Will and left him to sort out the bar, the kids and everything. So, this is your empire, eh? I never thought you'd ever leave the bright lights and come back to this dump.'

'I'd had my fill of the bright lights. Really isn't all it's cracked up to be. I'm loving every minute of this. And I even have time to call my own again occasionally.'

'Time to socialise with the lovely Ben, I gather.'

'Not really. We just found our dogs were having a relationship and went along with them. As chaperones, you understand.'

'Now there's a new one. But I wouldn't blame you for finding any excuse. He's gorgeous. If I wasn't happily married . . . '

'Josie, you haven't changed a bit. Tell me, what do you know about our Ben Ciammo?'

'What do you want to know?'

'Anything you know. He buys flowers for someone. He says he hasn't got to get back to a wife, but he doesn't say there isn't a wife. I don't want to get involved, not if there is someone.'

'You should ask him, I don't think there's anyone in his life, but how would I know? He works too hard. He never brings anyone into the pub, until last night, that is. He does come in to eat quite a bit, which suggests he has no little woman at home, cooking him delicious Italian food. But, one never knows. Now, when are we going to have a really good natter? Catch up on everything?'

'I'm not sure. I work till six every day and you start work about the same time. Could be tricky.'

'Why not come round one evening, after you close the shop and have something to eat with me and the

50

monsters, and then once they're in bed we can have a drink and chat then. And I'll see what I can dig out about Ben. See if he is the ideal mate for you after all.'

Daisy grinned. 'Now that makes it quite irresistible. Seeing your kids, I mean of course. Can't believe that the rebellious Josie Robinson is a mum and chief cook and bottle-washer in a pub.'

'We all have to grow up sometime, I guess. Hey, why don't I have some of those daffs for the pub? Brighten the place up a bit.'

Daisy picked out several bunches and wrapped them. 'On the house,' she said with a grin.

'Don't be silly. You can't afford to do that. Here. I can always claim it on the tax.' She dropped a five-pound note on the counter. 'You can give me a massive discount but at least that's something towards the flowers. See you very soon. Oh, and that woman who was leaving when I came in. Watch her. She's a pain in the whatsit. Likes to think she's lady bountiful but she has a habit of ordering stuff and then never collecting it.

'Asked us to get her some special wine and then we were saddled with it when she decided it wasn't quite the right vineyard after all.' She swept out, leaving Daisy almost gasping for breath. She'd always been a live wire and full of fun.

★ ★ ★

It was almost lunchtime when Ben arrived in the shop once more. She looked up as his large frame filled the door.

'I'm sorry, but I've run out of people to buy flowers for, so I've come in anyway. Just wanted to make sure that Emma hadn't suffered any ill-effects after her plunge in the duck pond.' He looked down to see Emma about to leap up at him.

'Emma, what do you think you are doing? Get back in your basket immediately.' The little dog put her tail down and looked as dejected as only a Jack Russell could. She crawled back to her basket, as slowly as possible, obviously hoping the order would be cancelled.

'Poor little thing. Obviously under the thumb,' Ben said, a twinkle in his eye. 'Any chance of having some lunch with me?'

'I'm sorry, I couldn't possibly. I'm on my own and there are several orders I have to make up for this afternoon. Besides, I'm sure you have work to do yourself. You can't possibly keep leaving your own work for long periods.'

'I have people who keep things going. But you're right. I do have to work hard to keep up and the more time I take out in the day, the later I have to work at night. I spent a couple of hours in one of the greenhouses last night after I got back.'

'Really?' Daisy was surprised. 'But how can you work in the dark?'

'We actually have electricity, you

know. Lights and everything. Even living right outside the town, as we do.'

'It just seemed odd to think of a plant-grower working at night. It somehow sounds like a daylight-only job.'

'I love working at night, in the glasshouses. It's peaceful and calming. The smell of the earth and the silence make you feel at one with the world.'

'But ... well, isn't it a bit anti-social?'

'Do you have anyone to mind if you're a bit anti-social? Is that what you're trying to ask?'

'I suppose so. You were buying flowers for someone. I was curious. Especially as you seem to want to spend time with me.'

'And you're wondering if I'm free to do so?' He looked slightly irritated. 'I hope you don't think I'm the sort of person who would two-time anyone?'

It was Daisy's turn to look irritated. 'It's natural. I see a lot of people buying flowers for all sorts of reasons. I'm not accusing you of anything. Of course I'm not. But I don't know you. Not really.'

'I'm sorry about that. I thought we were getting to know each other, but I was wrong. I'd hardly be asking you out if I was seeing anyone else. I'm sorry to have wasted your time.' He swung round and stalked out of the shop.

'Ben, wait. Please. You . . . ' she tailed off. He had left and she could hardly run out after him. 'Blast,' she moaned. 'I really messed that one up.'

'You look as if you'd lost a pound and found a sixpence,' Barbara remarked as she came back into the shop. 'Is the next load ready to take out?'

'I'm sorry. I've got all behind. Not to worry. They didn't need the big hand-tied bouquet till four. A retirement presentation, I think.'

'Right. Well I'll do the other two bouquets, shall I? Daisy. What is wrong?'

'Nothing. Really. Sorry. I was just a bit upset about something. I said

55

something I shouldn't have said. Now, are you ready for a cuppa? I'll put the kettle on and it'll soon be lunchtime anyway.'

However much she tried to concentrate on what she was doing, the memory of Ben's kiss the previous evening was foremost in her mind. She really wanted them to be friends . . . or even something more. But now she'd blown it. She'd asked one question too many and he'd been offended. Silly, over-sensitive man.

Emma appeared and gave a little whine. Daisy looked at the little dog. It was almost as if she understood. 'Sorry girl but it looks like the end of your affair with Toby, too. Just shows the dangers of becoming attached to anyone. From now on, it's just the two of us. OK?' Emma's brown eyes looked up trustingly and her tail wagged.

★　★　★

For the next few days, Daisy kept herself as busy as she could. She followed up her various plans for making a website and began photographing every arrangement and bouquet she possibly could.

The next big event in the floral world would be Mothering Sunday. Everyone seemed to want to send flowers for that occasion and it was one of the biggest money earners of the year.

Being only her first few months in business, the experienced Barbara had filled her in on the usual routine and potential work. She had decided to take on another member of staff, on a temporary basis, to join them for the weeks leading up to the event. If only there was someone who could answer the phone, take orders and maybe even do some of the deliveries, it would be most useful in relieving the pressure.

'Anita usually puts the prices up for Mother's Day. Well, in honesty, the wholesalers do the same but as she used to say, it is a captive audience.'

'Well, I shan't. I'll try to cover the extra cost by doing some special offers. I'll get some of my pictures printed and blown up to make some posters. We'll do some children's specials too. Kids often like to buy something for their mums and I don't like to think of making a profit out of them.'

'That's a nice thought. But how will you stop everyone buying the cheaper stuff?'

'Put an age limit on it. Under tens only, or something. We'll make up one or two posies and cost them and then I'll take . . . pictures . . . ' She tailed off as she saw Ben approaching the shop door. Feeling suddenly flustered, she went into the back workshop, leaving Barbara standing staring.

'Good morning,' she said. 'Did you want to see Daisy?'

'Well, yes please. I have a large order to place. It's a bit of a rush job. Wedding flowers.'

'I see. I'll call her. She should be free

but I can always take your order if she isn't.'

'Thanks.' He looked distinctly uncomfortable, Barbara thought.

'Get rid of him. I don't want to see him,' Daisy protested.

'I can't. I won't. What ever is wrong with you? The man wants to place a large order. You can't afford to turn it away, just because of some stupid tiff you may have had. Now, get out there and see what he wants.' Daisy sighed and said nothing as Emma slunk out of her basket and went into the shop. She sat down on Ben's feet and stared up at him.

'Hello, little dog. Good to see that at least one of you is still speaking to me.'

'I'm sorry. We got off on the wrong foot the other day. You wanted to order some flowers?' Daisy said in a voice that shook so much that almost squeaked. Why did this man make her feel so unsure of herself?

'It's a bit of a rush I'm afraid. Can you do several arrangements and a couple of bouquets for Saturday? Oh and some buttonholes?'

'I should think so. What exactly did you have in mind?'

'Well, I don't know much about these things but I hoped you'd be able to advise me.'

'Of course. Where shall we start? I assume you are organising a special occasion? The floral arrangements . . . exactly how many is several?'

'I don't know. Enough to make the place look special.'

'I see. Maybe we should start with the bouquets. Are they a presentation? Hand-tied are very popular. Easy to simply put into water with no need for arrangement. Depends on the recipient of course. They can be quite heavy to hold. Elderly clients often prefer the more traditional. And you mentioned buttonholes.' Daisy stopped. Bouquets. Flower arrangement. Buttonholes. Her heart fluttered, totally out of control. 'Are we talking of a wedding here?'

'Of course. I thought your, er

. . . colleague had told you. I'm organising an emergency wedding.'

'I see. Then perhaps the bride would like to be consulted? It is usual for her to decide on the wedding flowers. Saturday, you said? Do you actually mean this Saturday?'

'That's right. She's leaving the whole thing to me. I said I knew an expert and she was very happy to leave it all to me.'

'And the emergency? Why is it all such a rush? I mean to say, we usually have several weeks notice for these things.'

'If you can't manage to do it all, just say. I'm sure I can organise something . . . someone else. I thought you might be glad of the business.'

For one desperate moment, she wanted to tell him to take his business elsewhere. To tell him to get lost and out of her life. But commonsense prevailed. She did need the business and to turn him down would be petty and childish.

'Of course, I'd be delighted to

organise the flowers for your wedding. I'll get out some photographs and we'll sort it all out. Now, if you'd like to take a seat over here, we'll see what we can do.'

4

They looked at pictures of bouquets and various table arrangements. Try as she would, Daisy could get no clues about colours or the bride's preferred flowers.

'We're having the ceremony at home. I've got caterers doing food and so the flowers are just to make the whole thing look more festive. It's a fairly small house and a very low-key affair, but I want it to look special for the bride. It's the least I can do in the circumstances. We could do with some of your fancy bows and perhaps you can trail bits or something around. What do you think?'

'I'm sure I can come up with something suitable,' Daisy managed to stammer. The tumult of emotions shooting through every corner of her body was making her feel quite sick. She was torn between wanting to tell

Ben to get lost, and to fling herself into his arms and tell him not to go through with it. She took a deep breath and swallowed back the bile she felt rising.

Professional, she told herself. Important to be professional. He was planning to spend a lot of money here and she had a reputation to establish. If she did a good job, she could get more such commissions, exactly as she had planned.

'Perhaps some small sprays with ribbons and greenery trailing would help. Do you have any high shelves, or picture rails? And colours? What colours are your rooms?'

'Oh heavens. I never realised this would all be so complicated. The walls are a sort of cream and the carpets are blue and cream. Oh, and there's a sort of peach colour too, in the sofas and chairs. And picture rails. We do have picture rails. But they're only narrow ones. Not proper shelves or anything.'

'That's fine. I can make loops to hang the sprays from them. Perfect. So, if I use cream and peach colours, that should do? I really ought to see the room first, but as there's scarcely any time, I suppose I should just go ahead. I'll supply stands for the pedestal arrangements, and hooks for the wall sprays of course. I'll bring them. Any particular colour for the bridal bouquet and buttonholes?' She kept herself busily writing notes and managed not to meet Ben's gaze. When she did look up, she caught his lazy smile, as if he knew exactly what she was thinking.

'Does the colour matter?'

Daisy gulped. 'Of course it matters. Most brides want to choose flowers within the slightest shade variation and I've known them to send things back if they don't match exactly. Heavens, it's the most important day of a girl's life.'

'I didn't realise. Sorry. I'm not allowed to see the bride's outfit, of course. But I gather the same colours would do. Let's go for the creamy thing again. That will fit with anything won't it?'

'I guess so. Unless she's wearing white.'

'I doubt that. She doesn't ever wear white. What other colour might she be wearing?'

'Well, cream I suppose. I'll go for cream, but you must promise to phone me if she doesn't like the idea of cream rosebuds, I'll go for rosebuds. They are usually the nicest looking. If you're really sure she doesn't want to be involved in something as important as her bouquet.'

Ben shook his head again.

'Do you want a large bouquet or a small one? What sort of size is the bride? Only if she's very tiny, a large bouquet can look overpowering.

'She's about your height. And dark. Bit like me. Shouldn't think she'd go for anything too large or extravagant.'

'Oh dear. I really should have met her. I don't like making these sort of decisions on my own and you're not really being a great deal of help.'

'Sorry. I only know about growing plants.'

'Right. Well, I think that's all I need to know for now. Perhaps you'll give me your phone number in case I need to check anything. Oh and your full postal address for the estimate. I'll work on it and get it in the post tonight.'

'Don't worry. With this short notice, I'll just have to bite the bullet and pay whatever the cost.'

'That's a bit of an invitation for me to rip you off isn't it?'

'I know I can trust you.' He glanced at his watch. 'I've a hundred things to do so I'd better get on. I can leave it all to you now, can't I?'

'Of course. I'll deliver and set it all up first thing on Saturday. I'd have preferred to do it Friday evening, but you intimated that wasn't practical?'

'Sorry, no. It'll be mad on Friday all day and there are various relations turning up during the evening. I've got someone coming in to clean on Friday. You know where I am don't you?'

'Yes, of course. And the bride? Where

do you want her flowers to be delivered?'

'To my place of course. She lives at my place. OK then, till Saturday morning. I'll make sure you can have the room to yourself and you can come as early as you like. We'll be up and about by six o'clock, if necessary.'

'I might as well come at that time. I still have the shop to run for the rest of the day and we're usually busy on Saturdays anyway.'

He took her hand and leaned down to plant a kiss on her forehead. She tried to think of it as just a friendly gesture but it felt as if he was pushing a sharp icicle into her brain.

She pulled back and forced a smile on to her frozen lips.

'You're my saviour. I knew you wouldn't let me down. Thanks a million.' He strode out of the shop as she watched. It seemed an empty and desolate place suddenly. Barbara put a cup of coffee on the table beside her.

'Thought you might need this,' she

said sympathetically. 'Sounds like you've got a whole lot to do in the next couple of days.'

'You're not kidding. I'd better start costing and then ordering the flowers. Three days notice . . . not exactly a well-planned wedding, is it? Can't think why they're in such a hurry, these days.'

'Oh, you think the bride's about to give birth, do you?'

'Shouldn't be surprised. Can't think of any other reason to organise this show at just a few days notice. Do you know, the bride doesn't even want to choose her own bouquet? I can't believe that. I wonder if she's even chosen her own dress?'

* * *

For the next hour Daisy sat at her desk, listing all the flowers she would need and the various bases and containers she would need. If it had been for anyone but Ben, she would have relished everything she was doing.

Taken pleasure in choosing and planning the flowers and how the final arrangements might look. After all, she was being given almost carte blanche to choose and arrange the entire floral display, no expense spared.

Whoever the client, she knew her reputation depended on her being completely professional about it all. She ordered the extra blooms, to be delivered on Friday morning, along with their usual order.

She would have to work extremely hard all day to finish everything off and would be relying heavily on Barbara to man the shop. If she prepared everything here, she could take all the arrangements ready to put in their places.

Many people arranged the flowers on site but that would take forever and with her special racks in the van they would all transport without damage. The final pieces to trail down could be added if she was careful. She bit her pen as she considered the tasks ahead.

'Do you think we'll manage in the shop on Saturday? I'll be at the wedding until well after we open here, even if I do go at six o'clock in the morning.'

'I should think so,' Barbara said doubtfully, her expression contradicting her assurances. 'I could see if my niece would like to come in for a few hours. She's only a schoolgirl of course, but she's got a good head on her shoulders and if nothing else, she could answer the phone. She wouldn't want much pay. A few pounds and she'd be over the moon.'

'That's a good idea. It can be hectic in here on Saturdays, especially if I've had a late night and an early start.'

'You'll be exhausted. I'll ask her tonight. Do you want to interview her first?'

'Course not. I'll take your word for it. Thanks Barb. Don't know what I'd do without you. We will have to think about getting more help once I get this place really on the map. If things go as I intend, there will be loads more weddings and special arrangements. We might even need another van.'

Barbara smiled at her enthusiasm and wished her luck. She was everything this town needed. Young. Passionate. Ambitious. A hard worker. Yes, Daisy deserved success and she was going to do everything she could to help her achieve her goals.

* * *

By Friday night, the cold room was bursting at the seams with the weekend flowers, several bouquets that had been ordered and all the flowers for the wedding. Daisy had felt her emotions running riot as she worked, torn between the beauty of the blooms she was working with and their intended purpose.

The buttonhole she had decided would be Ben's had the choicest rosebud she could find. Pale peach colours dominated the arrangements for the room, gerberas and carnations with the occasional exotic lilies to add scent and different colour tones. Dark green leaves backed the wall sprays to make a good contrast against the pale walls Ben had spoken about.

There were three large pedestal arrangements and a half a dozen small sprays to hang and trail, just as Ben had suggested. The bridal bouquet was made up of creamy roses, delicate and light. She felt very pleased with the whole collection.

'You've done them proud, love,' Barbara told her as they shut the door. They can't help but love them all.'

'At least I should be through the delivery relatively quickly. It's just a case of standing them all in place and hanging the small sprays. I must remember to sort out some hooks. I know I've got a load at home, somewhere.'

'Right, well, you should get home. Everything's organised here, ready for you to collect. Try to relax this evening.

You've got a big day ahead of you.'

'Thanks so much for everything you've done today, and I hope that your niece manages OK till I get here tomorrow.' She locked up, and feeling bone weary, went home and slumped down on her uncomfortable sofa. Emma crawled up beside her, sensing her mistress's mood. She rested her head on Daisy's lap and looked up, eyes bright and tail wagging very slowly.

'Oh Emma, you're such a comfort.' She felt like weeping. She cursed herself for allowing Ben to come so close to her. She should have gone along with her first cautions . . . someone as nice as Ben must have been involved with someone.

She forced herself to poke around the freezer to find some food, and put a fish pie into the microwave. Emma's bowl was quickly emptied and the little dog gave a woof of pleasure, as Daisy went to the door to let her out. 'Sorry girl. We're not going for a walk tonight.

You'll have to make do with the garden.'

The microwave pinged and she took out her meal. Though she felt hungry, it tasted like cardboard and after eating only half, she pushed it to one side.

The evening felt like an eternity. She put on the television and tried to watch a film but all the time, she kept seeing images of the huge family party at Ben's farm. She held a picture in her mind of the happy relatives and an excited gathering for the big day.

★ ★ ★

The alarm rang at five-thirty the next morning. It was still pitch dark and she shivered as she got up after a fitful night. Emma looked up from her basket at the foot of the bed as if she thought her mistress had gone completely mad and the little dog tucked her head back between her paws. It was just too soon to get up.

'Early start, girl.' Daisy laughed. After

a quick shower, she pulled on her clothes and added a fleece to her usual sweatshirt with its daisy logo. Still shivering, she padded down to the kitchen and made some strong coffee.

There was no-one around the town so early and she parked outside the shop to load the van. The postman waved cheerily as he passed.

'You're up bright and early. Some-one's special day?'

'Yes. You could say that.' He handed her the package of mail and she dropped it on her desk to attend to later.

The van was practically full to bursting by the time she'd finished loading everything. She added scissors, tape and a few extra sprays of greenery and other oddments she might need. For good measure, she also put in a few extra flowers, just in case, she told herself.

By seven o'clock, she was driving out to the farm. Lights blazed out of every window and she could see signs of activity out in the long rows of greenhouses.

She wondered if she would ever have a wedding herself. Probably not, she told herself. She always chose the wrong men. When she thought she might have found one, it turned out he was committed to someone else.

She pulled up in front of Ben's house and took a deep breath. She knocked on the door and fixed a smile on her face. A flustered looking woman opened it.

'Yes. Can I help you with something?'

'Daisy Jones. I've come to do the flowers.'

'Oh, yes. Ben said you'd be here early. I'm a friend of the family. I'll just show you the room and you can get to work. Yell if there's anything you need. I'm up to my eyes in helping the bride. She's acting like someone about to have a nervous breakdown. This is the main room. We shall be opening the doors between here and the dining-room when the caterers have set up. Did Ben say he wanted any flowers for the dining-room?'

'Well, no. Not really. But I'm sure I can stretch what I've brought. Oh, what a lovely room.'

'Yes. I think so. Well, as I said, I need to get back to the bride,' She rushed out and Daisy heard her pounding up the stairs. She looked around. It was indeed a lovely room. Bigger than one might have expected from the outside of the house.

She opened the doors through to the dining-room and saw that the space would seem twice the size when they were pushed back. A small table covered in a white lacy cloth was waiting for the wedding cake and a long table stood at the side of the room.

Daisy frowned. She really needed to put her arrangements in both rooms to provide continuity. Perhaps with the extra greenery and taking a few flowers from here and there, she could stretch her decorations a little. She went out to the van and began to unload. Emma whined but was confined to the front seat, right out of harm's way.

Daisy worked hard, carrying the basic pedestals, the arrangements and the several boxes of small sprays. The bouquet and buttonholes, she left stored on the higher racks until later. Once there was a little more order in the house, she would find somewhere safe to leave them. At last, everything was unloaded and she closed the doors at the back of the van. At least Emma had settled down, she thought gratefully.

'Ah, you made it,' Ben's voice called from the doorway. 'Got everything you need?'

'Good morning. Hope you are a bit less nervous than the bride.'

'Certainly am. I've just been out watering the greenhouse. Nothing stops even for a wedding.'

'Bit like having animals to look after, isn't it?'

'Speaking of animals, have you brought

Emma? I haven't seen Toby for ages.'

'She's safely locked in the van. I'm not letting those two rampage around, not in the midst of all this.'

'I'll leave you to it. Can I organise some coffee for you?'

'Thanks. That would be great in a little while. I need to work for a bit longer before I stop.'

Daisy studied the room. It was extremely tasteful with subtle colours picked out in the sofa and chairs. Her flowers were well chosen and the peach and cream shades with complementary greenery were perfect against the light walls. She stood two of the pedestals between the larger pieces of furniture, and the third she placed in the dining-room, close to the cake table.

Immediately, there was a much more festive look and she began to hang the wall sprays with their swags of delicate green trailing leaves and ferns. She had brought the picture hooks to hang them and everything was working out perfectly. With the spare bits she had brought, she was able to put a couple more in the dining-room and even provided a small table decoration. She was personally, delighted with the effects.

'Wow, that looks wonderful,' Ben called as he came into the room carrying two mugs of coffee. 'You're a genius. Hope you've charged me enough. Looks as if you've done quite a lot more than I asked for. I forgot the dining-room would be part of the whole thing. You've saved the day. My sister's wrath won't fall on me after all.'

'Your sister?'

'She's the highly-stressed bride. I'm keeping well out of her way.'

'Your sister? But I thought . . . well . . . '

'You thought it was my wedding? Sorry. I suspected that was at the back of your mind. Couldn't help teasing you a little.'

Daisy stood open-mouthed. The rush of emotion charging through her body was most unnerving. It was as if she's been reprieved from a life sentence.

'I'm sorry . . . ' she managed to stammer. 'Is that coffee for me?' She snatched at the mug and swallowed quickly, hoping the liquid would calm her and stop the shaking she felt was making her look an idiot.

'No, I should apologise. I wasn't sure if the way I feel about you was just one-sided. If it mattered to you that I might be getting married, then I felt it might mean you cared just a little. That it wasn't just our dogs that was bringing us together.'

'How could you? I've been feeling really . . . well. I . . . ' She was struck by a thought. 'Did you ever find Toby?'

'No. Maybe he's lurking somewhere around your van . . . sensing Emma or something. I must admit, he's usually very much more high profile, especially when things are happening and there are people around.'

She went cold. She had left the van door open for some time when she was unloading. Could he have sneaked inside?

The bridal bouquet and buttonholes were still in there. She thrust her half empty mug into Ben's hands and rushed out.

She pulled open the back doors and there indeed was Toby. He was lying curled up with his nose touching the back of the racks. Emma was on the other side, her own nose as near as she could get to her beloved friend.

'Now if that isn't true love,' Ben said gently. Toby lifted his tail and wagged it. Emma gave a whine. 'Maybe they could come out for a little run?'

'As long as they aren't allowed in the house, anywhere near my flowers. I'll get the bouquet out now and we can take it inside.'

'That's gorgeous,' he said when he saw the delicate cream roses. 'Beth will love it.'

'So, why was all this such a rush?'

'Beth's fiancé is being posted to the Far East unexpectedly. They decided that she should go with him. It's all so much easier if they are married, apparently, so hence the haste. They've been together for a couple of years and always planned to marry. Just hadn't got round to it.

'His company preferred to send married couples on overseas assignments. They leave on Monday, so today was the only day possible. Sadly, my parents couldn't make it but there are a couple of cousins representing the family and there'll be lots of friends.'

'They live in Italy, your parents?'

'Yes. They had other commitments and with such short notice, couldn't make it.'

'But they must have been gutted to miss out on their daughter's wedding.'

'They're busy enough. We'll send them pictures and videos. Well, I'd better see how things are going. I'll take Toby inside now, if I can catch him.'

'And I'd better get back to the shop. Barbara and her niece are holding the fort.'

'Couldn't you possibly leave them to it and stay for the wedding? I'm sure Beth would be delighted and she'll want to thank you for the excellent job you've done with the flowers.'

'I'd love to, but I'm afraid duty calls. I've left too much to Barbara already this week. I'll see you some time.'

'Do you want a cheque?'

'I'll send you the bill later. I'm sure there's quite enough to keep you busy today.'

She scooped up her little dog and thrust her into the van. After checking her displays once more, she collected the various bits and pieces and left them to their celebrations. The caterers were drawing up as she left and she knew a whole new round of activity was beginning. She felt a pang of disappointment, not to be a part of it all but she had done her bit and had the rest of the day to look forward to.

'So, how did it all go?' Barbara asked cheerfully. She was staring at Daisy's expression, trying to find out exactly what was her mood.

'Fine. I really needed more wall sprays than I took. Ben forgot to mention that there were actually two rooms being used. But, I took some extra greenery and a few more flowers so I made up some more. It all looked lovely.'

'Crikey. You must have been up at the crack of dawn.'

'Well, before it cracked actually. It seemed weird being here to load up before six o'clock.'

'You seem more cheerful than I was expecting. Considering.'

'Considering what?' Daisy asked ingenuously.

'Well, you were rather taken with Ben weren't you?'

'Maybe. His sister will no doubt make a lovely bride. I didn't see her as she was upstairs panicking, by all accounts. But I gather there's a family resemblance so I expect she's very beautiful.'

'His sister? I see. That explains it.'

Daisy grinned and went through to the back workshop to see what was needed.

'Hello, Daisy,' said the young girl who was standing awkwardly staring at various vases of flowers. I'm Barbara's niece, Nicola. I was just wondering what I'm supposed to do with this lot.'

Daisy smiled and held out her hand. Once the introductions were over, she showed the girl how to treat the ends of the flowers in near boiling water to stop them from wilting.

'Wow, you'd think it would kill them wouldn't you?'

'It seals the bottoms and stops the air bubble from escaping, keeping the stems upright. There. Now you can take them through. Have you been busy?'

'Not too bad. Auntie Bee has kept me busy doing all sorts of chores.'

'I see. Hope it wasn't too boring.'

'No. I quite enjoyed it really. I'd like to do some serving though. If I'm allowed. Just the easy stuff.'

'I'm sure you'll soon pick up the tricks of the trade.'

The shop bell kept ringing during the day, enough to keep the three of them busy and ensure the flowers sold out. It was very satisfactory and with the profit from the wedding and other sales, made Daisy feel very gratified that she was on the right track for making her business a success.

'You've done very well,' she told Nicola at the end of the day. 'I'd like you to come again next Saturday. I shall need extra help when Mother's Day looms. It's going to be a very busy time and the more experience you get, the more help you will be.'

'That's brill,' Nicola said enthusiastically. 'I enjoyed myself and getting paid as well, that's really a good deal.'

5

'Hang on a minute,' called a voice from outside as Barbara was pulling down the small window blind over the door.

'I'm afraid we're closed,' she called back.

'I need to see Daisy.' Barbara lifted the blind and saw Ben outside. A large car was parked half on the pavement, its lights flashing. She opened the door, calling out as she did so. Daisy came through and stopped in her tracks.

Emma rushed out and gave him the enthusiastic greeting he'd hoped to get from Daisy. 'I've come to collect you for the evening party. We've got a disco and loads more friends arriving. You have to come. I insist.'

'But I'm feeling shattered and I need a shower more than anything.'

'I'll take you home and you can

shower and change. You've got ten minutes.'

'But I can't . . . '

'Course you can,' Barbara insisted. 'She's coming. I'll lock up. Get off with you and take your dog with you. I dare say Ben will have somewhere for her to stay.'

Bewildered, Daisy found herself packed into the strange car, her bag and Emma on her lap and Barbara waving enthusiastically from the shop doorway.

'Beth insisted that I fetch you. This is her new husband's car, in case you think I've suddenly come into money. Now where exactly do you live?' Feebly, she gave directions and groped for her key.

'I'll get you a drink while you change. What have you got? You look in need of something.'

'I was up pretty early this morning,' she protested. 'I'm worn out.'

'Nonsense. I was probably up earlier than you and I'm still going strong. OK. You go and shower. I'll find something for you to drink. And I'll feed Emma.'

When she was out of the shower and wondering what on earth to wear, she heard Emma's feeding bowl rattling round the floor. Ben had obviously found the dog food. She pulled on some smart black pants and a turquoise silk blouse. It would have to do. Not exactly what she might have chosen, given time. She brushed her damp hair and fastened her favourite gold necklace round her neck.

'Hope I'll do. Best I can manage in the allotted time. Oh good. You found the wine.'

'Drink this. You'll feel better. And yes, you'll do just fine. In fact, you look wonderful. Where's the weary looking woman I collected from her shop a few minutes ago?'

'I left her in the shower.' She laughed, taking a glass of ice-cold wine. 'Mustn't drink too much. I can't remember when I last ate anything. It's been a long busy day.'

'We have champagne, asparagus rolls, smoked salmon and tons of other stuff, so come on. Let's hit the road.'

'But I need to exercise Emma. She's been inside all day.'

'She can spend the evening with her boyfriend in the barn. It's quite dog proof. They'll be fine and I'm sure they'll run around like idiots once they're together. Now let's get going. I'm missing out on this expensive food and entertainment I've laid on.'

* * *

She felt nervous as they drove to Ben's home. She would be going into a family gathering and she was a stranger. She felt as if she was prattling on, to cover her nerves.

'Ben doesn't sound very Italian. Nor does Beth for that matter.'

'English versions. It's much simpler.'

'I'm sure both names sound wonderful in Italian. I hope some of the guests speak English.'

'Stop worrying. There's only a very small contingent from Italy and they all speak perfect English. Now, ready?'

It was well after midnight before Daisy even sat down. Ben had kept her busy meeting everyone, eating, drinking and best of all, dancing. He was a superb dancer, most unexpectedly, she thought. He moved with a grace and totally natural rhythm that made her feel as if she too was dancing well. Beth and her new husband had greeted her with such pleasure that she was wondering what they had been told about her. Far from feeling she was intruding on a family occasion, she was made to feel like one of them.

'Thank you so much for the wonderful flowers. Ben said you were talented, but I never expected anything like this, with such short notice. You must have worked like crazy to get so much done.'

'They don't call me Crazy Daisy for nothing,' she said, her words slightly blurred by a mixture of tiredness and the champagne she'd been drinking.

'I shall look forward to seeing what you come up with for your own wedding,' Beth said teasingly.

'My wedding? I don't have plans for any weddings.' She felt her colour rising.

'Come on. One more dance and then I'll possibly allow you to rest.' Ben swept her away in his strong arms. The music had become softer and the pace slowed almost to a standstill. She felt her partner's arms tighten around her and she seemed to be floating somewhere close to the stars.

His breath was warm against her neck and his lips brushed her cheek. She closed her eyes and waited for his mouth to find her own. She never even noticed that the music had stopped and that people were moving away. She was lost in a world inhabited only by her and Ben.

There was a ripple of applause and she jumped. She opened her eyes and found they were surrounded by a laughing group of friends and family.

'You guys just broke the record for the longest kiss without a breath,' one of the men called out. Daisy blushed and wished the earth would open beneath her feet.

'Do you blame me?' Ben called back. 'You're just jealous of my good fortune. Dancing with the most desirable woman in the room.'

'Just watch it,' Beth hissed. 'This is supposed to be my day.'

'I'd never even try to compete with you, Beth. You look stunning,' Daisy said honestly. The cream silk suit was perfect and complemented her dark hair. She was a very beautiful lady.

'Yes, but she's not only my sister, she's a married woman. Besides, I'm the good-looking one in our family.'

The banter continued and Daisy enjoyed the happy relationship the brother and sister shared. She felt sad to think she was an only child and must have missed out on so much.

She could scarcely take her eyes off this man, totally captivated by his easy charm and kindness. He was obviously hard working and very caring. He was perfect husband material, she realised. Then she tried to pull herself together. The excitement of the occasion and the romance of it all were turning her into a mush. She was behaving in a ridiculous manner as if she were some idiot teenager having her first crush on some pop star.

'I think it's time I was leaving. Can you get a taxi for me?' she asked.

'I'll drive you home,' Ben insisted.

'You've had far too much to drink,' Daisy retorted.

'Not at all. I've been drinking mineral water most of the time. I wouldn't risk it otherwise. Besides, I have to make the most of using this big flashy car owned by my brother-in-law, while the opportunity's here. It's back to the Land Rover tomorrow.'

'Then I'd better find Emma and we can go. Thank you so much for inviting me to join you and I wish you every happiness in your new life.' Beth pulled her close and gave her a hug.

'Look after my little brother for me. I know we're going to see much more of each other in the future. He deserves some happiness after all he's been through. Just don't hurt him, promise me?'

'Of course not,' Daisy stammered. 'But what do you mean? After all he's been through?'

'Oh. Nothing. I didn't mean anything. Just look after him.' She swung round to say goodbye to her other guests and left Daisy standing waiting for Ben to return.

They drove home quietly. Toby had come along for the ride and sat in the back with Emma. The pair curled up together like puppies from the same litter. When the car stopped, they stood up, waiting for the next move.

'I expect you'll want to get back,' Daisy said.

'Coffee would be nice. And I rescued some of the cake to have with it.'

'OK. Come on in then. And you'd

better bring Toby, as long as he promises to behave.'

They sat side by side on the sofa, eating the squidgy chocolate cake. 'Unusual to have a chocolate wedding cake.'

'Best we could do in the time. Besides, who wants the right fruit cake when there's chocolate available?'

'Ben, what did Beth mean when she said you'd been through a lot?'

'Living with her all my life I expect. It's been tough at times. But I'm fine. Honest, reliable and beginning to feel I've found my way in life.'

'What do you mean?'

'Nothing. Nothing at all. If you've finished eating and drinking, I should go. Let you get some rest. You look exhausted.' He removed the plate and mug and drew her close. 'You really are a very lovely person as well as beautiful, Daisy.' His lips on hers re-kindled the surge of emotion she had felt when they were dancing.

Her heart was saying the words she

dared not say aloud. 'I love you Ben Ciammo. Ridiculous as it sounds, I love you.'

'I'll call you,' he said as he rose from the sofa.

'Night,' she whispered, just before he went through the door. He tucked Toby under his arm and raised his other hand in a farewell gesture. Daisy lay back on the sofa, so weary, she fell asleep right where she was. Emma snuggled close, tucking herself behind her mistress's knees and the pair slept until eight o'clock the next morning.

* * *

When Daisy awoke, she felt stiff and confused about why she had slept on the sofa. As the memories of the previous day filtered back into her mind, she grinned. The relief that had swept over her when she realised that it wasn't Ben's wedding after all, the day spent working the shop, the unexcited pleasure of Ben collecting her from work and finally, that wonderful wedding party.

Best of all, she hugged the memory of Ben's kisses. She was in love. But did he really love her? She frowned as she remembered Beth's words. He'd suffered something . . . been through a lot, according to his sister. But he would tell her nothing. Perhaps it was something too painful to talk about.

All the same, Beth had been encouraging about the possibility of some sort of future. If there was some secret, it surely couldn't be too bad or she would have said more.

After a lazy morning, Daisy was beginning to feel better. She'd had a late breakfast and lots of coffee and was trying to decide what to do next, when the phone rang.

'Daisy? It's Josie. Are you busy?'

'Oh, hi there. Not really. Why?'

'I'm cooking a late lunch for us all and wondered if you'd like to join us. Have to be around two-thirty, after we close the pub.'

'That sounds great. But aren't you tired? I mean don't you need to rest?'

'Course I do but obviously you've never had kids. Rest is a word that people dream about and never actually realise. See you later then. Come whenever you like. You can always have a drink first.'

'Thanks. That's really kind of you.'

* * *

Daisy was really pleased at the prospect of an afternoon spent with her old friend and she looked forward to meeting Josie's children. She wondered if she should take the dog but felt it might be a bit of an imposition. Instead, she would take Emma for a walk and collect the van from work and leave the little dog sitting in it, outside the pub.

It was a chilly day, with threatening rain clouds hanging overhead. She pulled on an anorak and put a change of shoes and a dog towel in a bag.

Emma was delighted at the prospect of a walk and leapt around in a frenzy of excited yaps.

They walked to the park and from there, back to the shop. She let herself in and wandered through to the back. Everything was clean and tidy, nothing out of place. It was her own little empire. Perhaps one day she would own several shops like this. A whole chain of them.

'A Daisy Chain.' She laughed. There were scarcely any supplies left for the week, she realised. They had sold so many extras in addition to the wedding, they needed a large order to replenish things. She also needed to get to grips with the approach of Mother's Day. It was only two weeks away and she had done nothing towards her great plans for a range of inexpensive arrangements for children to buy.

'Blast,' she suddenly remembered. 'I forgot to take any pictures of the wedding arrangements.' She glanced at her watch and impulsively, grabbed her camera. If she hurried, she could get to Ben's house and probably take some pictures before the arrangements were taken down or deteriorated too much and she still would make it to Josie's in time for the late lunch.

Ben's house was silent. She couldn't see anyone around and assumed most of the guests had already left. She hoped there would still be someone at home to let her in. She rang the bell. After an age, Ben appeared round the side of the house.

'Well, well. I didn't expect to see you today. Thought you'd be fast asleep for most of the day.' He leaned towards her and kissed her mouth. She could hardly help but kiss him back.

'I wondered if I might take some pictures of the flowers. I forgot in all the hurry yesterday.'

'Oh. I'm sorry but they've mostly gone. I gave them to various people who'd helped. I'm sorry, but I didn't think you'd need them.'

'Oh well. It was just an idea. I'm

planning to make a folder of my own arrangements for people to choose from. Instead of always using the Flower Network stuff. It seemed like a good chance but trust me to leave it too late.'

'There are still the wall hanging things. And loads of people were taking pictures. I'm sure we can get some of them copied for you. Oh and I forgot, the caterers were most impressed and wanted your card. Seems they're often asked if they do flowers as well, so you may get some business from that too. I only had your number but I gave that to them.'

'Thanks, Ben. That's excellent. I'll just take a look to see if I can photograph what's left.'

'Why don't you stay and have something to eat? There's loads of leftovers.'

'I'd love to but I can't stop for long. Josie's invited me to lunch.' She regretted having to refuse his offer, but maybe it was as well to slow things down a little.

'She never invited me,' he moaned. 'And she cooks like a dream.'

'Used to be more of a nightmare, from what I remember, but you reckon she's improved.'

'Maybe I should give her a call and invite myself along too.'

'Don't you dare. This is a girl thing . . . we're going to talk about our lives and loves and hopes. Will is being commissioned to look after the children while we catch up. I'll see you some other time.'

They arranged to meet one evening and walk the dogs together. Though she didn't really want to leave him, Daisy knew it would be foolish to rush into anything more too quickly. They needed to get to know each other better and besides, she wanted to see if Josie had found out anything about him, as she had promised she might. Mind you, she thought, after being so involved in his sister's wedding, she probably knew more about him than Josie, anyhow.

It was a lovely afternoon, and

certainly Josie's cooking skills had improved beyond recognition. The two boys, both under five were quite a handful but both Josie and Will obviously adored them and the doting father took them off for a walk.

'There's some bread on the side. You can feed the ducks,' Josie called after them.

'That takes me back. I used to love feeding the ducks when we were kids. Probably the same progeny as the ones we used to feed.'

'Probably. Now, can I get you a brandy or something? Then we can settle down to a proper gossip.'

'Nothing thanks. I'm really full. That was a smashing lunch. Much better than we ever cooked for old Miss Flynn.'

They were soon into a flood of memories, laughing at silly things they'd done and the way their lives had gone.

'So, what's going on with Ben?' Josie asked.

'Well, his sister was married yesterday and I did the flowers.'

'Yes, I know. We supplied the booze. They did ask us to go to the party after we'd closed but we didn't have a baby-sitter and frankly, we were just too exhausted. Did you go?'

'After the shop closed, yes, I did.'

'And?'

'And I enjoyed it. She's a lovely lady. Hinted of something in Ben's past but I couldn't get him to talk about it.'

'He's quite a private person isn't he? I never did discover anything much. Nobody seems to know much at all. He's either carefully hiding something or else he's squeaky clean. The only thing I do know is that his parents started the business and when it wasn't doing too well, they went back to Italy. I suppose his sister didn't go with them. She worked away most of the time.

'I never realised she actually lived at the house. It was all a bit secretive and very sudden. Nobody could give me any proper details. It was all hushed up.

Money was very tight . . . I don't think they actually went bankrupt or anything. It's only what it is now because of Ben's hard work and determination. People think very highly of him. They don't gossip about him at all.'

'Maybe that's it then. He had a row with his parents and that's the big secret problem. They weren't at the wedding. But you know what these Italian families usually are, for sticking together.'

'Dunno. I suspect there's more to it. But if you're getting so close, you can surely ask him?'

'I guess so. I'm trying to take things easily for now.'

'You really fancy him, don't you? Not that I'd blame you. If I didn't adore my Will, I'd give you a run for your money.'

'You would too. I had a bad experience before I left London.' She poured out the problems she'd had with Ray and why she'd left to come back to her hometown.

It was a couple of days before Ben

called round to the shop. He collected the bill for the wedding flowers and then suggested a walk that evening. Daisy agreed and they planned to meet near the common. By the evening, it was pouring with rain and their plans had to be abandoned.

'You could come round to my place and I could cook something. I'm not brilliant but I can manage a decent pasta,' Daisy offered. As soon as she put the phone down, she realised what she had said. She had just offered to cook pasta for a real Italian who was probably weaned on the stuff and whose mother probably spent half her life making it from scratch.

The best she could do was to buy the fresh stuff from the supermarket and produce a half edible sauce from various packets and cans. Maybe she could change the menu, if she had time to go out to the shop and buy ingredients.

'Do you mind holding the fort for a few minutes?' she asked Barbara.

'Course not. Can you get me the new TV magazine? I forgot to get it this morning.'

'Sure. Won't be long.'

When it came to it, she did buy ingredients for her pasta sauce after all. Why should she be ashamed of it? If he didn't like it, he needn't eat it.

*   *   *

In the event, he thought it was great and they sat cosily in the little kitchen, a candle and bottle of wine between them.

'I was a bit embarrassed, cooking pasta for an Italian. I expect your mother made it all by hand didn't she?' He looked away.

'Mother was too busy with the business to do too much cooking.'

'I see. She worked in the nursery then?'

'Sort of. Actually, it was always a bit of a moot problem. She worked but wasn't really up to the business aspects of it. Dad wasn't in the best of health and when the business failed, they decided to go back to Italy. I've just about cleared off the debts and we're now starting to make a decent profit. In fact, this year, things are definitely looking up.'

'That's good. Must have been tough for you. Weren't you tempted to go back with them?'

'And leave debts behind? Of course not. I wouldn't want to go back there anyway. I'm more English than Italian now. I can barely hold a conversation in Italian these days. Much to my mother's disgust.'

It was a pleasant, companionable evening, with no pressures. When it was time to leave, Ben held her close and kissed her tenderly. There was no demand in his manner and she felt happy, peaceful and comfortable with him.

'I'll see you soon,' he whispered as he left.

She thought about the enigmatic

man. Admittedly, she knew very little about him. She knew why he was working so hard, but did she know any more about how he felt about things? Was the problem spoken of by his sister simply that of his parents debts? Somehow, she didn't think so.

6

'There's someone to see you,' Barbara called one afternoon when Daisy was working on the computer in the office. She was trying to get her Mother's Day publicity organised and time was very short.

'Who is it?'

'Wouldn't give a name,' Barbara said right behind her. 'Some bloke. Says he knows you.'

'Oh dear. I'm right in the middle of these posters. I have to get them to the print shop before the end of the day. I suppose I'd better come. Rescue me if it looks like going on. Make some excuse about an order or something.' Barbara smiled and nodded her agreement.

Daisy went into the shop and stopped when she saw her visitor.

'What on earth are you doing here?'

'I might ask the same about you. What on earth are you doing in a place like this? Is this really why you gave up everything?' Ray stared scornfully around the little shop and reached for Daisy's hand. He pulled her towards him and tried to kiss her. She ducked away. 'Don't you even have a hug for an old friend?'

'Not really. We were hardly friends when you kicked me out.'

'I didn't kick you out. You chose to leave. It was a bad time. Look, can't we go out for a drink or something? We need to talk.'

'I'm sorry, but no. I can't leave the shop in the middle of the afternoon. We always get busy as people are starting to go home.'

'I thought you were the boss? Surely you have someone to take charge for a while? The woman who came through to fetch you? Can't she manage? Or can't you trust her?'

'Of course I trust her. I'd trust her with anything, but I don't actually want to go anywhere with you. We have nothing to say any more.'

'Excuse me,' Barbara interrupted. 'The order you were waiting for? It's just come through on the machine.'

'Oh, fine. I'll see to it right away. Ray is just leaving.'

With an expression that defied any challenge, Barbara stood guard over the door to the office and Daisy went through it, hoping the trembling in her knees wasn't too obvious.

Seeing the immaculate Ray again had caused just the slightest flutter in her heart . . . more a slight feeling of panic, she realised. He'd always manipulated her and she knew she had to stand up to him.

The shop bell rang and she heard someone come in. Barbara went to serve them and she prayed that Ray had left.

'Daisy, please talk to me.' She swung round.

'Get out of here. This is my private office.'

'I can understand your not wanting me to see the extent of your so-called empire, but I do need to talk to you. I want you to come back to me. Come back to London and live with me again. There's a vacancy coming up in the office there. You could probably get your old job back. Think what you used to earn and the life you had. You can't possibly choose to die here in this dreadful backwater. I love you Daisy. I miss you. Come back with me.'

'Ray, I'm flattered. Truly I am. But I don't care for you any more and I certainly don't want my old life back. I love it here, however much of a backwater you might think it is. This is my home now.'

The shop bell rang again. The customer going out. Another murmur of voices. Someone else was in the shop. More than one person. Daisy heard Barbara's voice.

'I need to go. Barbara has customers waiting. I won't let people be kept waiting.' She got up and pushed past

116

him. There were two people waiting. She apologised and went to serve one of them.

'You OK,' Barbara asked. 'Do you need me to get help?'

'I'm OK. I can handle this.'

'I'll see to the rest of the customers. Call me if you need me.'

When she went back to the office, Ray was sitting in her chair, looking at the computer screen.

'What's all this?'

'I'm doing some posters for some ideas I have.'

'Looks good. You still have a flare. Daisy, I really mean it. I miss you so much. I need you back with me. Please think about it.'

'No Ray. You hurt me very much. Made me think all you wanted was my contribution to your grand plans for a lifestyle change.'

'Don't be silly. It was all a misunderstanding. I love you. Always did.'

'So, did you buy your expensive apartment?'

'Course not. Not without you. It was all for you.'

'Yes, like I'd believe that. So you're still in your old place?' He looked away. Daisy stared at him. There was obviously something wrong. 'So, what are you really doing here? What do you want? And don't tell me you only want me. Come on. Honesty time.'

He turned back to her, an expression of misery clouding his face.

'I've lost my job. Everything's gone.'

'Good heavens. What on earth did you do?'

'Nothing much. You know what it's like in the media world. One minute you're flavour of the month and the next you're out on your ear.'

'Quite. And you suggested I'd consider returning to that sort of uncertainty.'

'Well, you at least chose to resign. You could get another job at the drop of a hat.'

'And the job that may be coming up, the one you mentioned? It wouldn't be yours, I take it?'

He shrugged. 'Daisy, I need your help. I'm behind with payments on the flat. If I don't get some money soon, I've had it. I shall lose it. Can't you help me out? For old times sake?'

'I could lend you a few hundred at most. I'm sorry. Everything I have is tied up in this place and my own flat.'

The shop doorbell rang again and Daisy looked up nervously.

'A few hundred would be good. Just till I'm settled in something else. But I really mean it. I want you to come back to me. I do really still love you Daisy. There's never been anyone else since you left me.'

Another ring of the shop doorbell. It had been going fairly constantly but this time, the door was shut with a slam. Barbara came through looking worried.

'What is it? Is something wrong?'

'That was Ben. He was coming through to the office and I couldn't stop him. He must have heard what you were saying and whatever it was, he was obviously very upset by it. Went out as if he was being chased by the hounds of hell. And one of the hounds is still peacefully at your feet,' she tried to joke.

'And just who is Ben?' Ray demanded.

'Someone I know. A customer,' she said trying to make this interview less difficult.

'Ben. I see. So he's the reason you came back. How long was that going on?' Ray's handsome face took on an expression of ugliness. 'Actually Daisy, I need much more than a few hundred. If you're not willing to come back and earn a decent salary, forget it. You've obviously given up on yourself and what you could make of your life. I need someone with something to offer.'

'You're not worth wasting words. Just get out will you? I have work to do.'

He turned and left the shop noisily. Daisy put her head in her hands and sobbed. The emotional strain of seeing the man she had once planned to marry had taken its toll.

Barbara came in with a cup of tea. She said nothing but left it beside her young boss, knowing she was best left alone for a while. Eventually, Daisy sipped the now cold tea and went through to her stalwart helper. 'Thanks Bee,' she murmured. 'Sorry about all that.'

'I gather he was the reason you left London?'

'You could say that. What a sleaze. I can't believe I once thought I loved him.'

'Good-looking sleaze, I must say. Shame Ben overheard. He left a cheque, by the way. Said thanks for everything as he went out.'

'I hope that isn't what I thought it was. Sounded like some sort of goodbye. I'd never go back to that other life. And I'd certainly never go back to Ray. He hasn't changed one little bit. Still the same, totally selfish man.'

'You should go and find Ben. Say

thanks for the cheque at least.'

'I'll see. I'll think about it anyhow.'

★ ★ ★

The following week was very busy with the approach of Mother's Day. Life became totally absorbed with flowers. Orders had poured in all week and they had bought in huge amounts of extra blooms for the occasion. Daisy was making arrangements in her sleep and they even had to work on the actual Sunday to get everything delivered in time.

The children's arrangements were a huge success and even Barbara's niece, Nicola, was pressed into making up new ones as they quickly sold out. They were still working at four-thirty on the Sunday afternoon when the final orders had gone and the final clearing was left.

'Please go home now, Barbara. Your husband will think you've deserted him forever. We should be quiet tomorrow

122

so we can catch our breath. You must take a half-day at least tomorrow to make up for the extra time. I'll pay you overtime of course. I'd never have coped without you and Nicola.' She made up her mind to buy a special present for her treasured helper to thank her for all the extra effort.

'I've really enjoyed it, Daisy. Honestly. When I think of how it used to be before . . . all profit and no real love given, it made such a difference. And as for overtime, well Anita used to assume we did it for love not money. Everyone was really pleased with the way you handled it. Well done. I reckon things are going to go really well from now on.'

After all the excitement, the next few days were miserable for Daisy as the absence of Ben in her life began to hit home. She completed her work with a lack of enthusiasm that she despised. Barbara was quite worried about her and constantly tried to persuade her to visit Ben.

'It's up to him. If he wants to see me he can phone or call in at the shop. Heaven knows, he was here often enough before.'

She lost count of the number of times she picked up the phone to dial his number and put it back again. She drove to the end of the lane leading to his house on several occasions but then turned round.

She had walked Emma on the common in the hopes that he might do the same and they would meet accidentally. She neither saw nor heard anything of Ben. She tried to tell herself he was just busy. After all, now his sister had left, there must be loads of extra things for him to do.

The third Saturday after the wedding arrived and she kept remembering the wonderful time they had shared. She wasn't sure how she would get through the next day. She was supposed to enjoy a day off, not dread it, she told herself. She needed to tell Ben that the conversation he had overheard meant nothing. That Ray was out of her life forever.

By late on the Sunday afternoon, she made up her mind that she simply had to see Ben, whatever the outcome. He must be told the true facts about her and Ray. He had obviously overheard some of the conversation . . . enough to scare him off but he needed to know the whole story.

She dressed carefully, wanting desperately to convey the right message. Not too casual, nothing too formal. She brushed her hair till it shone and clipped it back from her face. She rubbed her pale cheeks, hoping to bring a bit more colour to them.

'Come on then, Emma. Let's do it.' The little dog of course was delighted they were going somewhere. Anywhere. As long as her beloved Daisy was going, she wanted to be a part of it. She drove her van to Ben's house and pulled up, her knees still feeling decidedly shaky. She left Emma whining in the van and rang the doorbell. She couldn't believe he was out.

After all the effort she had made to force herself into this visit, he wasn't here. Just as she was about to leave she heard a yap and Toby came tearing round a corner, barking furiously when he recognised the van and scented his friend inside. His paws scraped frenziedly at the door and Daisy opened it, if only to leave a little of the paintwork intact.

'Oh, it's you. That explains why Toby suddenly behaved like the maniac he truly is. How are you?' Ben's tone was formal and his usual smile absent.

'I'm OK. How about you?'

'All right I suppose. You're on your own?'

'Well, yes. Except for Emma, of course.' She shouldn't have come, she thought. He isn't pleased to see me. 'I . . . I just came to thank you for the cheque. You were very generous, but you needn't have added the extra. My bill was quite fair.'

'Beth insisted. She said you'd done far more than you needed and she wanted me to add the extra to thank you.'

'Thank you again then. Have you heard from her?'

'They phoned from somewhere exotic to say they were taking a few days holiday before they settled back to work.'

'Right then. You're obviously busy. I won't keep you.'

'I'm just doing some potting.'

'On a Sunday afternoon? Don't you ever take time off?'

'Only if there's something worth taking time for. Do you want to come and look round the greenhouses? If you've nothing better to do? You were interested once.'

'I'd love to, if you've got time.' She hoped the shaking of her legs wasn't too obvious.

They walked into the warm greenhouse where he had been working. Rows of tiny plants were growing in pots, stretching endlessly along the racks the full length of the huge house. The smell of damp earth filled the air and she sniffed appreciatively.

'Goodness, this must take forever. What are they? They look like begonias.'

'Full marks. I'm trying a few lines in flowering plants for bedding or even as houseplants. It's certainly labour intensive but I enjoy the peace of it all. It's also creative in a way. Making something out of such tiny seedlings is very positive.'

'I can imagine. Maybe I could sell some of them in the shop. Especially if you produce flowering houseplants.'

'I'm planning large scale distribution but maybe you could take a few. Preferential rates of course.'

'I'm sorry. I wasn't asking for a discount. I'd just like some decent stock. African Violets are always in demand for example.'

'They're in the other house. Come and look. I've got some unusual varieties. Bit of a hobby of mine. I like the idea of turning a hobby into something profitable.'

'Bit like me really.' He smiled and her heart turned over, quite out of control, it seemed.

Feeling much happier now, she followed him into a smaller house, slightly cooler and darker. He put lights on and they wandered along rows of so many different shades of pinks and purples, she was quite astounded. 'I've never seen so many colours. They're wonderful.'

They wandered back to the office at the end of the greenhouse and she perched on the edge of the desk. He gave her some commercial pictures to look at and they discussed business for a few moments. He wrote some notes in a ledger and she glanced round. The office was tidy and workman-like, as she would have expected.

'If you're seriously interested in stocking some of my plants, does this mean you're not going back to London? Only I thought . . . Are you going back to London? To your boyfriend or whatever he was?'

'He's my ex. There's no way I'd ever move back with him. He's selfish, unscrupulous, manipulative . . . '

'That's great. But I get the picture,' Ben interrupted. 'I'm so glad. I couldn't help overhearing him talking to you and . . . well, I thought you were tempted. I thought you were about to sell the shop and disappear from Brindley altogether.'

'You obviously didn't listen for quite long enough. I sent him packing. I was quite proud of myself actually.'

Ben leaned over and took her hands. 'I'm so pleased. I thought I'd lost you. I know we haven't known each other for very long but I hoped we would, well, have something more ahead of us.'

Daisy grinned and reached up to kiss his lovely mouth. The light danced in his dark eyes again and she knew there might be hope for them, possibly love for them, somewhere ahead.

'I'll make you some tea if you like.

Shall we go into the house?' She nodded and eased herself down from the bench. She noticed the photograph pinned to the notice board near the office door.

'Who's the little boy?' she asked.

'He's Marco.'

'Marco? He's a lovely little boy. Who does he belong to?' He was obviously a relative with the same dark hair and dark eyes as Ben.

'Marco's my son.'

'Your son?' Daisy gulped. 'But where is he? I don't understand. I mean, where does he live?'

'He's in Italy. It was a terrible decision to have to make but I can't look after him properly. I had to let him go back to Italy.'

Daisy felt as if the ground was swimming up towards her. She gripped the bench and took a deep breath, trying to stabilise her thoughts. So this was Ben's secret. He was actually married and had a son. However lovely a child he might be, it was a dreadful shock and made all the difference to their future together.

How on earth could Beth have encouraged her to become close to her brother when she must have known about this? It seemed clear now. Everything was clear. No wonder he didn't want to talk about himself. No wonder he wanted to keep quiet about his past, his life.

She rushed out of the office, yelling for Emma to come. Ben stood still, his face pale and his eyes troubled. The little dog responded, hearing something in her tone of voice. She leapt into the van and with only a small sigh, lay down on the passenger seat. Toby stood wagging his tail, barking softly as they drove away.

She almost wished she hadn't tried to sort things out. Now she knew the truth, it certainly didn't make her own future look any happier. Ben had a wife and child living in Italy. For whatever reason they had separated, she couldn't forgive him for not telling her.

7

When Barbara saw her the next morning, she felt shocked at Daisy's appearance. 'Whatever happened to you?' she asked. 'You look as if you haven't slept.'

'I didn't. Not much.'

'I'll make a drink and you can tell me about it, if you want to of course.'

When Daisy poured out the whole saga, Barbara's voice dropped. She put a comforting arm round her boss's shoulders. 'I'm so sorry, I should never have encouraged you to go and see him. But it's better that you know, before you, well make any sort of commitment. I knew there was something funny about him. Never quite seems to be properly up-front. But you'd think someone would have known about it wouldn't you? Something like that.'

'Well, now you know. Don't spread it

around will you? I shouldn't have told you really but I needed to get things off my chest. It isn't that he lied exactly, just didn't tell me the whole truth. He may be divorced I suppose, but how could he just let someone take away his son? I couldn't bear the thought of losing a child of mine, whatever the circumstances. And I could never settle with someone who couldn't tell the whole truth. I've been there before.'

The day seemed to pass very slowly. Everything seemed like very hard work and though she kept a fixed smile on her face for customers, it slipped away the moment the door closed behind them. She constantly told herself it was for the best that she had never told Ben how she felt about him and tried to be grateful that nothing serious had happened between them.

Maybe she should consider going back to London . . . even seeing Ray again. After all, he did say he'd changed and that he still loved her.

'Would you be able to manage on

your own, one Monday?' she asked Barbara.

'Course I can love. You want a day off do you?'

'I was thinking I might go to London on Saturday, after we close. I could stay over till Monday and be back the following day.'

'Do you good to have a break. Better make it soon though. Easter's coming up and we always do a good trade for Easter. People seem to want a lot of the spring flowers and there's usually a call for arrangements to be delivered. After the Mother's Day success, you've got a bit of a name for quality and fair prices.'

'Right. Thanks for the warning. Maybe I'd better leave my trip till later then.'

'If you go this weekend, it should be all right. There's still a couple of weeks to go after that. Seeing anyone in particular?' Barbara asked.

'Not really. Just some old friends. Thought I might look in at my old company too. See everyone and hear the gossip. I need a bit of a change.'

Daisy wasn't going to say more. Not at this stage. Her plan was really to test the market. See if there really was anything around on the job front, as Ray had suggested. She might even see him again. Could he possibly have changed as he'd said? They had once enjoyed each other's company and maybe she had overreacted when he'd called so unexpectedly.

It had been a shock seeing him like that. Maybe she was really out of place here and should consider returning to her old life. She had a few days to decide. To change her mind. Several times over, no doubt.

'There's someone on the phone for you,' Barbara called as Daisy was rearranging several vases in the window display for the umpteenth time that day.

'Can't you take a message?'

'It's some catering company. Want to know if you can do flowers for a silver wedding at the weekend. Their usual people have let them down. Saw your work at Ben's sister's wedding.'

'Oh. Right. I'll come. Thanks, Bee.' She picked up the phone. 'Crazy Daisy. How can I help?' Five minutes later she had the order for two large table arrangements and a pedestal. 'That's great isn't it, Barbara? We're getting a reputation and with it comes the orders. Now, I'll need to check the bases we have in stock. Must be getting low and with Easter coming up, I must be sure we don't run out. They want shades of pink, blue and silver. Have to use leaves for that and . . . '

She picked up the florist supplies catalogue and began to go through the options, making notes as she did so. Barbara smiled and went back to the shop to tidy something. It was nice to see Daisy getting enthusiastic again. Hopefully, she would forget all about the trip to London and seeing whoever it was she was planning to see.

As she worked, Barbara's mind was churning. She needed to do something or the florist's might close, she might lose her job, and Daisy would disappear forever. It was all important of course, but the thought of losing Daisy as a friend was by far the worst.

The door opened and Josie came in. Barbara grinned. This might just be the answer. Quietly, she took Daisy's friend to one side and began a whispered conversation. Josie nodded and they smiled conspiratorially. One way or another, they would do something between them. After all it was hardly interfering. They were simply protecting people they cared about and trying to make things right between them.

'I wanted a few fresh flowers for the bar. What do you suggest?' Josie said loudly, once they'd finished their plotting.

'The carnation sprays are good value. Last for ages.'

'Bit boring but you're probably right. Make up a bunch will you? Daisy not here today?'

'I'll see if she's free. She's working on

costing an order for the weekend. Glued to her computer no doubt.'

'Hi, Josie. Thought I heard your voice. Have you got time for a coffee? Come through.' Josie and Barbara exchanged conspiratorial winks as they passed each other.

'That would be great, if you can spare the time.'

'Did you know Ben had a child?' Daisy asked bluntly. Josie gasped and looked as if she'd been drenched in cold water.

'No. Didn't even know he was married. I'm so sorry. I never heard anything about that bit of gossip.'

'Can you believe he didn't tell me? I mean to say . . . '

'Have you confronted him? He doesn't seem the sort to play away. Surely not. You need to talk to him. Ask him for the full story.'

'I doubt I shall ever see him again. In fact, I'm beginning to think this whole move was a mistake. I should never have come back here. Nobody should ever try to go back to somewhere they've left.'

'Oh, for heavens sake. Don't be such a drama queen.'

'Someone else once called me that. But I'm not. Josie, I really thought we had something special. I even thought I loved him for a few moments. Showed how little I know about anything. Men in particular.'

'Why don't you come round for a drink. I'm in the bar on my own tomorrow night. The darts team's playing away so we'll be really quiet. Will's going with them and we have other staff coming in, just in case the kids play up. You can have supper with me, too. Pub grub of course, but it's not too bad.'

'Thanks. I might just do that.'

'I shall look forward to having a friendly face over the bar. I get so bored when it's quiet. Now, didn't you say something about coffee?'

Daisy went back to her planning as soon as Josie had gone. When she had finished the estimate, she phoned back to the caterers. They were pleased with her figures and immediately placed the order.

She took down the address for delivery and made a note of the times they were needed. She put the phone down with a satisfied smile. This time, she would remember to take pictures before the flowers left the shop. She had done nothing more towards her website or the brochures. Maybe she should forget about the London trip and simply use the time at home to work on her plans and ideas.

'You look happier,' Barbara told her later in the day.

'I've thought things through a bit. I'm not going to London after all. I might still take a day off on Monday though. I have some plans I need to follow up and well, I was thinking, I came back here with no-one special around me and so why are things any different just because I feel a bit let down?'

'Good. I'm pleased you feel that way. I'd hate it if you left here, just when things are going so well with the business. Have you done the order for Thursday?'

Daisy set to work and faxed the order to the suppliers. This weekend would probably be fairly quiet with a couple of weeks to go before Easter and apart from the special order, there wasn't too much else planned. It would be a good time to work on her ideas.

'Was Josie OK?' Barbara asked innocently.

'Fine. As you well know. You were talking to her, weren't you? I'm going for supper tomorrow night and to have a drink with her.'

'That's nice. Do you good to have a natter.' The older woman hid her face and grinned. Their plan was right on course. Provided Josie could persuade Ben to be at the pub as well, everything was set.

★ ★ ★

Daisy arrived at the pub soon after seven the following evening. The bar was empty and Josie was polishing glasses. 'Thank goodness someone's arrived. I was just wondering if I should go and fetch my knitting.'

'You? Knitting? Don't believe it.'

'Metaphoric knitting then. I hate trying to pretend to look busy when I'm not. Now, what can I get you?'

'Lime and soda please. I'm driving.'

Josie poured the drink and came round the bar to sit by her old friend. 'I put a cottage pie in the oven for you. Hope that's OK. I can cook anything else you'd like of course, but I thought that was easy and we could talk while you're waiting.'

'How are the boys?'

'All three are fine, thanks. Will's the most trouble, of course. Gets very involved with his darts team. Like a big kid himself.'

They chatted for a while and Josie went off to get the pie.

The door opened and Ben walked in.

'Oh, hello,' he said hesitantly. 'I wondered if you might be here.'

'Really. Why was that may I ask?'

'Saw your van outside. I nearly didn't come in, but I wasn't sure if you'd set this up . . . or . . . '

'Josie and Barbara. They were whispering together in the shop yesterday. I should have known. It's those two trying to interfere. How dare they?'

'At least stay for a drink.'

'I'm just finished thanks. Give my apologies to Josie. Tell her something came up and I had to go.'

'Daisy, wait. Your meal's ready,' she called as she came from the kitchen. Please come back.'

'Give it to Ben. He's a more deserving case no doubt. His wife's left him in case you didn't know. How dare you interfere with my life? I thought better of you. In future, mind your own business and keep out of mine. I should have known . . . you always did like to organise everyone. Well, this time you went too far.'

She glanced at Ben and saw his stricken face staring back at her. He looked as if someone had punched him. He took a breath as if he was about to speak, but decided against it and turned away. He pushed past her and flung the door open.

Tears welling, she stormed out behind him and went to the van. She opened the door and to her horror, Emma immediately leapt out. She ran straight to Ben's Land Rover and jumped up at the side.

Daisy saw Toby at the rear window and knew this was the reason for her own dog's disobedience. Ben couldn't possibly have seen her as he moved off, sending the small Jack Russell flying into the air. She landed with a thump, her eyes closed and body completely limp and unmoving.

Daisy stood screaming, unable to move. Ben must have heard her and stopped. He turned to see what the noise was all about. He leapt out and ran over to the dog. Toby was howling, trapped as he was inside the Land Rover. Sobbing, Daisy went to her pet and saw the blood streaming from one leg.

'Is she dead?' she asked, her voice choked with emotion.

'She's still breathing, but only just,' Ben said. 'I'm so sorry. I didn't even see her.'

'She must have been trying to get to Toby. I need to get her to the vet right away. I don't even know a vet,' she said helplessly.

'There's a rug in the back of the Land Rover. We can lift her on to that and I can drive you. We perhaps shouldn't move her, but I think we need to get attention right away. My vet lives above the surgery. Can you call him Josie? Butler, he's in the book. Tell him we're on the way.'

'Course I will. Hope she's all right. Let me know, won't you?'

Daisy held Emma as carefully as she could, trying not to move her and cause more injury. The rug was supporting her as they drove along the narrow lanes. Toby was whining in the back, as if he was trying to say he understood and wanted to help.

'She's such a little dog,' Daisy moaned through teary eyes. 'Didn't stand a chance against a great vehicle like this.'

'I'm so sorry,' Ben said again. 'I really didn't see her.'

'It wasn't your fault. I don't blame you. She jumped out of my van and ran straight into you. She was completely at fault. Even so, she doesn't deserve to die. She hasn't moved since I picked her up and she's scarcely breathing. Do hurry, please. I can't bear it if she dies.'

'I daren't drive any faster. We need to keep her as still as possible. Not much farther.'

After what seemed like a lifetime, they stopped outside a large house with a vet's sign on the gate. The lights were all on and the vet was waiting for them.

'Someone called and said you were on the way. Jack Russell I gather. Bring her in.' Daisy opened the door and Ben rushed round to take the dog from her. He lifted her and carried her straight to the surgery.

'Careful,' Daisy ordered as Ben gently placed Emma on the table. The vet unwrapped the blanket and frowned. He placed his stethoscope against her chest.

'Breathing's pretty ragged but it's there. Look, I'd prefer it if you waited outside. It's distressing for you to be in here and I need to examine her very thoroughly. She isn't conscious so you don't need to hold her and she can't feel anything.'

'But . . . she's my little . . . '

'Come on, love. Do as Mr Butler suggests. It's best this way.' He took Daisy's arm and led her out into the waiting room. She paced up and down, cursing herself every now and again. 'Stop blaming yourself. It was an accident,' Ben said over and over.

'But if I hadn't opened my door like that she would never have got out. She never does things like that. If I hadn't been in such a temper, it would never have happened.'

'And if I hadn't been in such a hurry to drive off . . . We could go on and on. You underestimate the power of love, even for two Jack Russells.'

'Love. That's a fine word to use. What do you know about love?'

'Perhaps you might let me explain at some point. I know you think I let you down but you really don't know the whole story.'

'Not for want of trying. You're not an easy person to get to talk. But not now, Ben. I can't take in anything now. Not till I know about Emma. She's probably my very best friend, you know. Little dog. She's only young and it isn't fair if she should die because of this stupid accident.'

There was a howl from outside and Ben smiled gently. He went to collect his dog, knowing he too wanted to know how his friend was getting on. Toby went straight to Daisy and sat on her lap. He licked her nose as if he was trying to provide some comfort and then sat quietly with the humans, waiting for the vet to come out of his surgery. It was the longest wait of her life, Daisy was certain.

'What on earth can he be doing in there?' she kept asking.

'At least we know she's still fighting. If the news was bad, he'd have come out to tell us. He must still be working on Emma, so that has to be worth some comfort.'

It was after ten when Mr Butler finally emerged. He looked exhausted but he managed a smile.

'She's got a badly broken leg and some damage to her ribs. But as far as I can tell, the lungs haven't been penetrated. We have to wait for a day or so, to be sure she hasn't got any other internal damage. I've X-rayed what was possible but it's hard to be certain of everything with such a small animal. I had to set her leg but as it was badly torn, there is quite a lot of stitching.'

'But you think she'll be all right?'

'As far as we know. The next few hours are critical.'

'Can I see her?'

'She's heavily sedated but of course you can look at her. Don't expect her to respond to you though.'

The little procession went into the kennel area behind the surgery. Toby led the way, stepping gently over the slippery floor. He whined gently when he saw Emma and sat down in front of the little cage, his head resting as close to his friend as he could get.

'Looks like they're good friends,' the vet said to Ben.

'She was trying to get to him when I hit her.'

'Strange how animals behave at times. Sometimes wonder if they're not wiser than us.'

Daisy looked up at him. She was kneeling on the floor staring at her little pet. Tears streamed down her face. 'Goodnight, little girl,' she whispered. 'Sleep well and get better for me. I'll see you in the morning.' Gently, Ben took her arm and lifted her to her feet.

'Come on. There's nothing we can do here. We'll phone first thing and we'll be over later on.'

'I'll need to collect my van, please. Perhaps you wouldn't mind taking me back to the pub?'

'Maybe you'd prefer to come back to my place? There's plenty of space and you might like company instead of being on your own.'

'I'll be fine. Just let me get the van. I want to be able to go over to the vet's first thing.'

She sat huddled in her seat and Ben drove carefully back. She was still shaking inside and the thought of someone looking after her was very tempting. When they stopped in the car park, she tried to get out of the Land Rover but her fingers were so numb, she couldn't pull back the door catch.

'Look, I'm sorry but you are not fit to be driving anywhere. You're still in shock. If you don't want to stay at my place, then I'll drive you back and sleep on your sofa. I refuse to leave you alone. Now, which is it to be? Your place or mine?'

'That's an old line,' she said feebly.
'Yours it is. More room, I guess.'

Ben's place was an old, stone-built house. Daisy had seen only the main reception rooms when she had done the wedding flowers and had merely glanced into the kitchen. They went in through the back and the kitchen was warm and welcoming with an Aga giving out comforting warmth. There was a kettle on the back and very soon it came to the boil. Ben made tea and poured it into mugs. She sat with her hands wrapped round it as if drawing the heat to revive her numb fingers.

'I'll just go and put some heat on in your room. Actually, it's really Beth's room but you can sleep there.'

'Thank you. You're being very kind.'

'For someone who's abandoned his family you mean?' He turned and left her staring into her mug of tea.

What on earth was she doing here? She wasn't even supposed to be seeing Ben, let alone spending the night at his house. But the thought of her own empty flat with no little dog was just too much to contemplate.

'Not now. Oh Emma,' she whispered. 'Don't die. You have to pull through.'

8

When she awoke the next morning, Daisy was totally confused. She had tossed and turned for hours and must finally have fallen asleep near dawn. The whole dreadful episode of the previous evening flooded back into her mind and she flung off the duvet, leaping out of the unfamiliar bed.

She pulled on her jeans from the previous night and ran down the stairs to get to the phone. She could smell coffee and there was definitely bacon frying.

'Can I use the phone please? And what's the vet's number?'

'It's OK. I called first thing. She's holding her own and he thinks she's out of immediate danger. He suggested we phone again around midday and all being well, you can go and see her. Sit down and I'll give you some breakfast.

One egg or two?'

'I couldn't. I mean, I don't eat breakfast . . . more than a piece of toast, that is. It does smell good though.'

'You didn't have any supper last night. You stormed out of the pub leaving Josie holding it in her hands, as I remember.'

'With good reason.'

'So you think. One egg or two?'

'Just one, thanks,' she said meekly. She realised just how hungry she felt, now the news about Emma was better. How could she be angry with him after he had been so kind? All the same, her current gratitude did not excuse his earlier lack of communication. 'Then I'd better get my van, if you don't mind driving me to the pub. Barbara will be wondering what on earth has happened to me.'

'Can't you leave her to cope for this morning?'

'Not really. I've got heaps to do and I shall be taking time out later to see

Emma. I expect she'll need quite a bit of nursing once she's home. I'm not sure how I shall work things out.'

'Well, I've been having some thoughts about that too.' He placed a plate of bacon, eggs, mushrooms and tomatoes in front of her. He topped up her coffee and pushed the toast rack closer to her. 'Eat up. We'll talk later.'

'Thanks. You are too good to be true it seems. This looks wonderful.' They ate quietly, both relishing the savoury food after the long fast. Now there was better news of Emma, she realised just how famished she was. When Daisy pushed away her empty plate, she gave a sigh. 'I really needed that, even if I thought I didn't. What were you going to say about Emma?'

'Why don't you come and stay here for a few days, just while she's getting over it? I'm here all the time and she would be well looked after during the day while you're at work. I can take her basket into whichever house I'm working and make sure she's safe and happy.

You can hardly have her in the shop. She needs rest and a lot of looking after. I dare say Toby will help. You can come round when you finish at the shop and we'll both have company.'

'I couldn't possibly,' she began to protest. 'But what would people think? I mean, your wife?'

'My wife? We'll talk about that later. Not now, not when we both have to go to work. I'll call for you later and we'll drive to the vet's. Your van will be fine where it is and I can drop you at the shop and pick you up. We'll go and collect some things for you. Tooth-brush, clothes and whatever else you need.'

'I need a shower and a change of clothes first. Before I go to work, I'll phone Barbara and tell her to open up and that I'll be a bit late. What time is it by the way?'

'Eight-thirty. Still relatively early, so you don't need to panic. So, what do you think?'

She pursed her lips as she thought

through his plan. Her heart was telling her she needed to get right away from him but he was certainly quite right about Emma. She couldn't look after her at the shop. Besides, he had promised to tell her everything she needed to know, hadn't he? Perhaps she was misjudging him.

'Well, yes. Thanks very much. You're quite right about Emma. It would be great to know she has the two of you looking after her. I don't deserve it after all the horrible things I said to you. You really are a very kind and thoughtful person.'

'I know. Just have trouble convincing the rest of the world. Now, come on. Let's get the day started. I'll dump the dishes in the dishwasher and we'll get you to your flat.'

The normality of the daily routine in the shop seemed very strange to Daisy. Barbara was horrified to hear about the dog's accident and immediately suggested she would mind the shop while Daisy went to the vet's.

'I can't. The van's still at the pub and Ben's fetching me later.'

'Good job we don't have any deliveries this morning, then.'

'Oh heavens. It shows my state. I never even considered that. Let's hope nothing comes in later this morning. I can collect the van at lunchtime, when I go to see Emma. Now, I'd better sort out what bits and pieces I need for this party on Saturday. Containers, bases, etc. Thanks for getting everything out for the shop.'

Several further orders came in for flowers for the silver wedding couple. They were destined to look like a florist's themselves, when the time came.

'At least I can deliver them all when I take the arrangements. Seems like they're providing us with some good business for the day.'

'We'd better add a few more things to the order, hadn't we? If you want to have anything left in the shop to sell, that is. And shall I ask Nicola to come in on Saturday? You'll be quite busy with these orders.'

'Good idea. Thanks. I'll go and phone the wholesalers right away.'

Barbara nodded and smiled to herself. At least keeping herself busy was taking away Daisy's worries about Emma.

She still felt slightly guilty that she had helped set up the meeting between her boss and Ben but Daisy seemed to have forgotten that, in all the fluster.

She heard the phone ring and from the conversation, knew it was Josie. She too seemed to have been excused for meddling, from what little she could hear. She also heard the news that Daisy was moving out to Ben's place for the next few days, while the little dog recuperated.

'Well, well,' she murmured. 'Who'd have thought it?' She busied herself with the vases and turned innocently to smile when Daisy came back into the shop. 'More orders?' she asked.

'No. That was Josie. Asking how

Emma is. I'm going to need to collect some stuff from the sundries wholesaler's this afternoon. Will you manage do you think?'

'Course.'

At one o'clock, Ben arrived. He was carrying two packets of sandwiches and insisted she ate as they drove along.

Emma was lying weakly in her little cage but her tail wagged when she saw her mistress.

'She's eaten breakfast and seems to be recovering well. She can't stand yet and I've had to give her more painkillers. I reckon she'll probably be ready to leave us tomorrow,' the vet told her.

'That's wonderful. Thank you so much. Thank you for everything you've done. I can't tell you how relieved I am.'

'Glad I was able to help. She's a lucky little dog. Much longer and I doubt she'd have made it. Good you got her here so fast.'

Ben drove her back to the pub and

she quickly went in to tell Josie the good news. She collected the van and with calls of see you later, drove off to the wholesaler's. She had only been there once or twice before and found the huge range of goods quite fascinating.

She piled her trolley with the necessities and took a look around to see what else was available. The collection of silk flowers intrigued her and she wondered if they ought to start selling them. The prices were very high and she knew the profits would be very scant. Maybe she could find a cheaper supplier and use them for all sorts of lasting arrangements and bouquets. It was quite trendy to have everlasting flowers these days.

Her mind raced and once more, she was able to forget about the rather difficult problems that lay ahead of her that evening. She and Ben were going to talk. She was about to discover the truth about his situation and possibly even which direction their future lay, if any, if indeed they had any sort of future.

Once the shop was closed and everything tidied away, she drove out to Ben's house. Toby rushed out to greet her and she laughed.

'No Emma yet,' she told him as he leapt around yapping with excitement. Ben stood at the door, watching. She went inside and stopped, sniffing appreciatively. 'Wow. Something smells wonderful.'

'I put a casserole in the oven. Nothing special. We need to talk. You should hear my side of the rumours before you make judgements. I don't know exactly what you've heard but obviously something has turned you against me. Just when I thought things were going so well.'

'That would be good,' she replied. 'I could do with changing out of my work togs though. Did you bring my stuff in?'

'I put it in your room. Beth's room. Supper will be ready in fifteen minutes.'

Feeling somewhat chastened by her

earlier behaviour, she went into the bedroom. It was a pretty, feminine room with lots of soft pastel colours and frilly drapes. It seemed slightly out of place with the rest of the house and not the sort of thing she might have chosen for herself, but she was very grateful for the use of it.

There was no real need for her to be there this evening, she realised, except that she did need to know more about this man and his family. She hung up the few clothes she had brought, brushed her hair and went down to the kitchen.

'Hope you don't mind eating in here,' Ben asked. 'Only it's much warmer and less formal.'

'It's very kind of you to put up with me and this food is great. Makes me feel ashamed of my own poor efforts the other night.'

He poured wine and served the casserole. 'My one-pot special,' he announced. 'Saves washing up and watching pans boil over.'

Once more they ate silently, neither

wanting to broach the difficult subjects that needed to be said. He made coffee and they stayed seated at the table to drink it.

'You wanted to know about my wife and son. Please understand this is very difficult for me to speak of, and this is the only reason I have never said anything before.'

Daisy smiled encouragingly and reached over to touch his hand. He drew it away and she felt slighted. 'I'll tell you the whole saga and then you can decide where we go from here.'

'My family decided to come over here, to England, when Beth and I were quite small. We hated leaving our old home and all the people we knew, to come to a cold country where everyone spoke some strange language. We soon picked it up though, once we went to school. My parents bought this property and began the market garden.

'In common with most Italians, they started with tomatoes and gradually expanded. When Papa became sick,

Mama took over most of the running of the place. Beth and I had to help of course and then a couple of distant cousins came over to help out while we completed our education. I wanted to go to university but it wasn't possible and so I took a course at the local college. Horticulture. I did come to love the work and still do.

'My cousin and I became quite close and eventually, much to the delight of our families, we decided to marry. I loved her very much and when we discovered she was pregnant, it seemed that our happiness was complete. The parents were thrilled and it seemed to give them a new lease of life. Our son was born and we named him Marco.

'Poor Leila became very sick herself and within two weeks of the birth, she died. It was devastating to us all. I hated the baby for a few days, knowing he had caused me to lose my wife but once the grief was passed, I realised what a precious gift I had.'

Daisy made a sympathetic murmur,

but he silenced her. 'Unfortunately, her death also was the start of a further bout of illness for my father. They knew the only thing they could do was to return to the warmth of Italy and get away from all the problems of running this difficult business. The property was mortgaged to provide them with enough money to buy a home back in Italy and they left.

'They took Marco with them so that Mama could care for him. I, as a young man with a business to run could hardly cope with a small baby, not on my own. Beth went with them but she hated the life, after all she had come to know here. She returned and lived here with me, as you know. So, Marco only knows he has a daddy of his own for a few weeks each year.

'He's now almost five and will soon be ready to start school. I dearly want to have him back here, but I'm not sure whether it's fair to him. Mama isn't getting any younger and she finds the work difficult. Papa also needs a great deal of care. I often wonder if I should sell up and go to live back with them.'

He paused and sat staring into his empty cup. Daisy cleared her throat, full of the emotions raised by his sad story. Could there be a happy ending she wondered?

'Thank you for telling me. It must have been difficult. I can't imagine how you could ever have parted with your little son, but I can see that it seemed like the only way.'

'I had to work very hard. Once I was in charge, I saw that the business was in a desperate way. Somehow, Mama had let everything slide and though we managed to get some money for them, the debts were quite incredible. I had to do everything myself and I suppose I was just so exhausted all the time, I didn't have enough time to grieve or even wonder what I was doing.

'But I got there. I'm now doing well and with certain specialisations, the future is looking good. I thought I knew exactly where I was going, till I met you. Suddenly, everything changed. You were there, filling the huge gap that was missing from my life.'

'Oh Ben, I'm so sorry. I jumped to a lot of conclusions that were quite wrong. You said things that made me think there was really someone in your life. When I saw the photograph, well I suppose I thought the worst. It seemed to confirm all my suspicions and insecurity. I was still smarting from my failed so-called romance as well. Didn't think I'd ever be able to trust anyone again.'

'So where do we go from here?'

'Where do you want to go?'

'I'd have thought that was obvious. I . . . I'm in love with you Daisy. I'd like to think you cared for me.'

'Oh I do, Ben. In fact, I have to admit, I've been in love with you for several weeks now. I was most upset when I thought I had a rival . . . no, more than a rival. I never wanted to hurt anyone and if you were married, then I was upset to think that you could be the sort of man to cheat. Not that you were as it turns out, of course.'

'I do come with baggage, of course. My son. I intend to make him a part of my life from now on. Do you think you could cope with that?'

'I need to think about it. It's a bit of a shock really. Of course I've known about him for a few days now, since I saw his photograph. I'm not quite sure I'm ready to be a substitute mother just yet.'

'Would you consider coming to Italy with me? To meet Marco?'

'Wow. I don't know. I mean, I'd be meeting your family as well. Wouldn't they resent me? Replacing your wife, which is what we're talking about isn't it?'

'They'll love you. How could they help it?'

'When do you want to go?'

'As soon as we can arrange it. How about Easter weekend?'

'Oh, but I can't. It's less than two weeks and it's a really busy time at the shop. And there's Emma. She won't be recovered enough to go into kennels.'

'Of course. I was forgetting.' He looked a little woebegone.

'I would like to come of course. It's important. But I need a bit more notice. Besides, it would be good to spend some more time together here, getting to know each other.'

Ben rose from his seat and went round the table. He took her hands in his and pulled her to her feet. He wrapped his arms around her slim waist and drew her close.

Their lips came together softly at first. They held each other close, their eyes closed and their minds filled with thoughts of the future.

* * *

Daisy went to work early the next morning. She wanted to get as much done as possible before the shop opened, to be quite ready for when the vet told her she could collect Emma.

172

She felt a huge sense of relief and could hardly wait for the call.

When the new flowers arrived, she quickly checked the invoice, skipping through the items as fast as possible. She pushed them into the vases with far less care than usual and took a chance that Barbara had done the sterilising of them last night. By the time Barbara arrived, the shop was all set up and everything in its place.

'Wow. I'm impressed,' she said as she came in. 'Did I get the morning off then and forgot about it?'

'Emma's coming home this morning and I wanted everything ready, so I can leave to collect her as soon as the vet calls.'

'Are you bringing her back here?'

'Well no. Actually, she's staying at Ben's place so he can look after her while I'm working.'

'But you'll miss her won't you?'

'Well, actually, I'm going to stay there too. Just until Emma's recovered.' Barbara's eyes widened.

'I see. So things are … OK? Between you?'

'I think so. We're taking things steadily. I may go to Italy to meet his family,' Daisy said casually. She was swept into Barbara's arms with a loud whoop of pleasure.

'When do you go? If you make it during the school holidays, Nicola can come in and we can run the place between us. I could have Emma to stay as well. Not sure I could manage Toby though. The two of them together are a bit much for anyone.'

'Don't get carried away.' She laughed. 'This is only the theory. Must say I hadn't planned on a family just yet. Especially someone else's child. It's a lot to take on.'

The phone interrupted the conversation and when Daisy heard the vet's voice, she was thrilled. She bounced out and told Barbara that she'd have to manage for the next hour or two. She was going to collect her beloved little dog.

Emma tried to greet Daisy with her usual enthusiasm but she wasn't quite strong enough. The vet gave her mistress a medical care sheet and a shield to put round her neck to stop the dog from licking her wound. There was also an envelope, containing a huge bill. She promised to send a cheque right away, having completely forgotten to take her cheque book with her.

'We're here,' she called, stopping at Ben's home. Toby ran out squeaking with joy at the sight of his little friend. 'Now Toby, Emma's a sick little dog so you have to be gentle with her.' The intelligent face looked up at her as if understanding everything she said.

'She'll soon be fine. Hello, little one. This is your new home for a while. Toby will look after you,' Ben said.

The two dogs walked together like an old married couple taking a stroll. The wild impulse to chase around was temporarily subdued.

'Barbara seems to think she and her niece could manage the shop for a few days if you want us to go away. She's also offered to look after Emma. So, if you want to book some flights, I'd be happy to come with you to Italy. We could go Easter Sunday if you can organise it that quickly.'

'That's fantastic. Thank you, my love.' He flung his arms round her and danced her along the path. 'I'll get my people organised here and phone my parents this evening. They'll be thrilled. I love you Daisy Jones,' he shouted. 'I love you.'

*   *   *

It was late October. Crazy Daisy had established itself as the leading flower shop in the small town of Brindley. It was number one for most occasions, and the staff of four and their boss were all good friends. On this particular Friday afternoon, chaos reigned. Everyone was rushing around, all trying to help with the same tasks.

'But I thought these anemones were

for the bridesmaids?'

'No, these are for the bridesmaids, those are for the tables.'

'Well someone had better sort them out and quickly. Daisy will be here in a minute and we don't want her thinking we can't cope. Is her bouquet ready?'

'In the cold room.'

'And the flowers for her hair?'

'Also in the cold room. Now just calm down everyone. Daisy needs us to be calm and organised. She's trusting us to do the first-rate job we all know we can do. We've got all the things we need and we have plenty of time.'

'You're right Barbara. Only we wanted everything to be the best. Perfect for her.'

'It will be. Now, Cathy, sort out those candleholders and put them in the box. Nicola, you can take the pedestals and put them in the van. We'll take both vans tomorrow and then we can carry most of the flowers ready in their containers, just to put round the room. The shop will be closed from eleven o'clock, with the large pictures in the window instead of the usual arrangements. I think just about everyone knows about the wedding.'

'I think the entire town knows about it. Here she is,' Nicola called. 'Stand by your places.'

'Really child,' Barbara scolded cheerfully. 'Hello love. Everything going to plan?'

'I think so. The parents have arrived with Marco and they're safely jabbering away in fluent Italian, none of which I understand at all. Still, not to worry. And we're meeting for our meal at seven. Josie's set up the back room so we can have a nice peaceful, all girls together evening.'

'Doubt we'll be that peaceful,' laughed one of the younger staff.

'Great. But promise me, none of the usual raucous hen-night stuff. I just want a nice, civilised evening. Otherwise, I'd have insisted on having it earlier in the week.'

'I'll keep them in order, don't you

worry,' Barbara promised. 'Or they'll all be looking for new jobs on Monday.'

At noon the following day, the bells were ringing in the little local church, the same one where Daisy had been baptised twenty-six years earlier. In front of friends and family, she and Ben exchanged their vows. Her mother and father, over from France, wiped away their tears. Radiant in a long, cream velvet dress, the bride wore a crown of tiny flowers and carried an elegant spray with some of her favourite daisies.

'You look wonderful,' Ben whispered as they walked down the aisle. 'It had to be daisies, didn't it?'

'Of course. You look pretty special yourself. If you weren't a married man, I could snatch you up and run away with you.'

'I might hold you to that. Now, there should be someone special waiting outside the church. Come on. Let's see.'

The two Jack Russells were standing almost to attention as the couple emerged into bright, if chilly sunlight. Both dogs wore smart new collars and leads and looked extremely proud of themselves.

'Emma looks a bit portly lately,' Daisy remarked. 'I hadn't noticed before. She must be getting too much to eat. Too many titbits.'

'I suspect there's another reason, Darling. I think they may have beaten us to it.'

'You wicked pair. I expect Marco will be delighted to have a whole litter of puppies to play with. It might help him to settle in.'

'I love you, Mrs Ciammo.'

'I love you Mr Ciammo.'

THE END

We do hope that you have enjoyed reading this large print book.

Did you know that all of our titles are available for purchase?

We publish a wide range of high quality large print books including:
Romances, Mysteries, Classics
General Fiction
Non Fiction and Westerns

Special interest titles available in large print are:
The Little Oxford Dictionary
Music Book, Song Book
Hymn Book, Service Book

Also available from us courtesy of Oxford University Press:
Young Readers' Dictionary
(large print edition)
Young Readers' Thesaurus
(large print edition)

For further information or a free brochure, please contact us at:
Ulverscroft Large Print Books Ltd.,
The Green, Bradgate Road, Anstey,
Leicester, LE7 7FU, England.
Tel: (00 44) **0116 236 4325**
Fax: (00 44) **0116 234 0205**

RHAPSODY OF LOVE

Rachel Ford

When painter Maggie Sanderson found herself trapped in the same Caribbean hideaway as world-famous composer Steve Donellan, she was at a loss what to do. She tried to distance herself from him, but he seemed determined to make his presence felt, crashing his way around the house day and night. Was there no way she could find peace from this man, or was he going to ruin her sanity too, as he had ruined everything else?

WHEN THE JOURNEY'S OVER

Judy Chard

Doctor Helen Elliot has gone to South America to persuade her father, Doctor Steven Elliot, to return to England with her. Helen meets Keith Denholm and they strike up a friendship. In Valdavero she goes to see her old friends Maria and Carlos de Cordobes and their adopted son, Manuel, her childhood sweetheart. But Manuel has vanished in very odd circumstances. Helen becomes involved in the search for him, high in the Andes among the guerrillas who have staged a spectacular kidnapping involving Keith.

DANGEROUS INTRIGUE

Karen Abbott

On the death of her father, Katherine Newcombe takes up a position in the household of a very respected family — but all is not as it seems in the Devonshire village. Miles Westcott, the schoolmaster, comes under attack when he investigates some of the strange happenings and Katherine herself is not left untouched by them. As Miles and Katherine draw closer together, the son of the local squire seems determined to force them apart, drawing them all into a dangerous situation.

HIDDEN MEMORIES

Joyce Johnson

For daring to disobey her antagonistic father, Bella Schofield was banished to Blackstone Grange, a bleak house on the North Yorkshire coast. She was housekeeper to widowed Harold Braithwaite and his young children. Initially hostile, the family soon warmed to Bella, but the isolated house had unnerving secrets. Only when Tom Windle, a radical young lawyer from London, visited Blackstone, could Bella finally unravel the mysteries of the house and her own strange background.